SHIFTING LOYALTIES

Book Seventeen of the Hayle Coven Novels

PATTI LARSEN

ALSO BY
PATTI LARSEN

The Hayle Coven Universe

The Hunted Series
Fiona Fleming Cozy Mysteries
The Nightshade Cases
The Clone Chronicles
The Diamond City Trilogy
Didi and the Gunslinger

and much, much more.
Find your new favorite author at
pattilarsen.com
Sign up for new releases
bit.ly/pattilarsenemail

CHAPTER ONE

"That's what *she* said!"

I choked on a French fry as Tippy's punch line made me blush and laugh at the same time. As outrageous as ever, the red-haired Hensley witch winked at me, substantial rack pushing the rude hand gesture screen printed on her chest into everyone's face. She'd forgiven me for choosing Shenka as my second almost as fast as she'd gotten over the fact Liam and I were an item. Sort of an item. I glanced sideways at him, found him blushing just as brightly as I knew I was and realized he'd never survive Tippy even if he were into her.

Hell, I still worried if he'd survive me.

Not going there, not right now. I'd had a nice, quiet fall and a lovely Christmas holiday at home. Meira even made an appearance despite her permanent relocation to Demonicon. Mom acted like herself again, young,

1

beautiful, enthusiastic. And though she still endured stress from her job, the control of the Brotherhood had been broken and her natural ability to balance work and home seemed almost eerie.

No complaining. I was just happy to have my mother back.

It felt difficult to return to Harvard for my last semester, to leave the happiness of my house behind, feeling, for the first time in ages, as though nothing changed since we first moved to Wilding Springs. Though so much had. Gram was the biggest indicator, quiet and withdrawn. Crabby most of the time, locking herself in her bedroom more often than not, her familiar touch in my mind so faint.

Broke my heart, knowing how much she suffered from the loss of her magic.

To Ameline of all people. I still owed that bitch for hurting my grandmother. Would kill her for it one day. Just as soon as my maji guide, Iepa, told me I didn't need the evil witch anymore.

Talk about a mood downer. I set aside my fork, shoulders slumping despite the giggling going on around me, the shuffling of other students, both witch and normal, coming and going. Talking, laughing, living. I wasn't really listening anymore. Besides, I felt tired, a little worn out. I'd let so many people down in the past, forgetting their problems, letting too much slide. No more. Which meant almost constant contact with a large group of loved ones. Regular visits to Austria to see Sunny and Uncle Frank, to the Sidhe realm to check in on the now single court of the Fey. The constant bickering between Seelie and Unseelie was always a treat.

The best part, though, were the almost daily chats with my sister, partly out of the need to keep her safe and partly because I just missed her.

And the coven. Always the coven. Shenka was great, better than great. I met her eyes as she rolled hers at me while Tippy brayed her excessive laugh. I loved my second, knew I'd made the perfect choice sneaking her out from under her sister, Tallah, though I wondered how she could stand the cold after growing up in California. Shenka insisted on joining me for every friend and family visit she could possibly attend, even trying to cross to Demonicon with me once. We both knew it wouldn't work out, her sad face peering at me through the veil from the basement when I crossed without her proving my point.

The only one who'd been able to join me on my father's plane was Charlotte, my bodywere. Which led me to believe she had demon ancestry somewhere in her wolfish makeup.

Thinking of Charlotte just made things worse. I still thought of her as "mine" even though she left me months ago, the bond between us broken. She came back from the dead for me, while, in hindsight, I thought she might have chosen to pass over in another circumstance. But then she'd left, with only a note in Ukrainian telling me she loved me. I hadn't heard from her in all this time. Yes, I focused on keeping an eye on those I cared about to be sure they were okay, but in Charlotte's case, she'd made it pretty clear she didn't want contact.

And no matter how much I hated the fact she was out there on her own, I had to honor that.

Mostly.

Shenka set aside her napkin, pushing away her tray. The dark, early evening sky pressed against the stained glass behind her, window rimmed in the frost of deep January.

"I'm off for home." Right, I'd forgotten. It was Friday already. We'd both acquired the habit of returning to Wilding Springs for the weekends. More family time. And while I looked forward to it for the most part, the idea of staying at school and getting some well-earned sleep seemed like a good idea.

No rest for the wicked.

Liam's hand fell on my arm as the small posse of girls rose. Donalda, tall and gray eyed, winked at me as she turned, one arm sliding through Tippy's to guide her away while Nicci blew us both a kiss, freckled nose wrinkling before mimicking Donalda's act, making a chain of witch girls as she linked up with Josie on the other side. It still amazed me at times I had real paranormal friends, people who understood me, the life I lived, because they lived it too. Looking up at the five beautiful girls made my heart happy.

Shenka paused, a sweet smile on her face, before turning her back to give Liam and me a moment.

Which made me nervous she knew something I didn't.

"I was thinking," Liam said in his deep voice, hazel eyes sparking with points of green as his cheeks pinked, tongue running nervously over his lips.

"That's got to hurt." I laughed, even more nervous, the giggling coming out a bit high-pitched. I squeezed his hand to cover my anxiety as he snorted. "Go on."

Liam relaxed, my irreverence seeming to put him at ease while my own butterflies beat their little wings against my ribcage. "You've been working so hard these past few months," at least someone noticed, "I thought maybe you could let Shenka go home this weekend." He paused. Swallowed. "Alone." Paused again while my chest tightened around those pesky insects. "So you could stay with me."

Oh.

Boy.

I'd been waffling over him, over what to do about us. Avoided anything involving making a commitment one way or another. Didn't help I only had a few months left before I was supposed to get married. Yeah, probably made things ten times worse. Still made me break out into a cold sweat and want to pack up and run for the hills just thinking about it. And while I felt pretty sure I'd be all over his sweet offer if the whole witching world wasn't in such a rush for me to find a husband, knowing the inevitable loomed made me squirm like a trapped rat waiting for the cat to pounce.

This was obviously some kind of bid on his behalf to spend some time alone and see if we could reconnect.

Shenka glanced over her shoulder, eyebrows raised. I knew then she was in full cahoots with Liam, but not in the way he thought. She waited, patient and 100% on my side, ready to support me no matter what I chose to do. As I looked back to Liam, the anxiety in his face, the way he bent his body toward mine, I thought of Gram.

She told me once he was too weak for me. That he was a terrible choice for a mate, a life partner. Her words held me back as much as my reluctance to bow to the pressure of centuries of witch law. Was it fair? No. At the time, I lost my crap on her, furious she would say such a thing. But the more I thought about it, the more her argument gnawed at my heartstrings.

And yet, there was only one way to find out if she was right. Which meant actually exploring this relationship at last. After all, I was running low on time. The coven law I had to be married by twenty-one loomed in my future.

I had to freaking choose already or step down as coven leader.

Images of other faces passed before me. Of Rameranselot, my demon friend who I knew now I'd never select to be my mate. But there were more, at least two more. One I pined for almost every day despite my best intentions. And the other I'd been trying desperately to free since August.

My appeals for the release of Sebastian DeWinter fell on deaf ears, both in my attempted communication with his queen, Pannera Sthol, and with Margaret Applegate, the leader of the European Council. Every attempt Mom and I made to discuss Sebastian's situation was ignored. I knew I could simply storm into the vampire mansion and take out their current leader, Celeste Oberman. Wanted to, so very much. Would enjoy watching her wither and burn in the sun. It was the very least I owed her after all the trouble the former Purity witch caused for my family.

But Mom insisted we use diplomacy despite both of us knowing Sebastian suffered at Celeste's hand, not to mention the rest of his clan. Anastasia, one of his lieutenants, already begged for my help, told me Celeste starved those she was meant to protect.

But my main concern centered on Sebastian. He was my friend, but more than that. He'd expressed his romantic interest at Sunny and Uncle Frank's wedding and, thanks to my immortality, choosing him was a distinct possibility. Yes, there were certain questions needing answers, such as if he was able to father children—blushing and having naughty thoughts—but no matter the truth, even if he was the perfect choice, I couldn't marry a vampire I couldn't reach.

That left one.

I just couldn't go there. To those chocolate eyes, that smirk. Delicious magic threading through mine. Creak of leather, the way his long, wavy hair hung, begging to be touched.

All of him. Begging.

Growl.

And snap. I shook myself a little as Liam touched my cheek with his fingertips just as Shenka's mind poked mine.

You suck at this, she sent with laughter in her mental voice. *I'll see you later.*

She left me there, a wave for Liam, as I pulled myself out of comparing the handsome, sweet guy in front of me to the other options I had for marriage like he was an under ripe watermelon.

What the hell was wrong with me?

"Sorry," I said, clasping his hands in mine. "Space cadet moment."

He bobbed a nod, started to pull away, his disappointment clear on his face.

"I understand," he said. "You have so much on your

plate. We both have responsibilities and the family has to come first. It was stupid for me to ask."

I tugged him back, forcing myself to relax. A weekend off with Liam? Okay then. Time to pull on my big girl panties and see where this went.

Ah. Unfortunate turn of phrase. Blush.

"I'd love to," I said.

And after the words left my mouth, I realized I really meant them.

Imagine that.

chapter two

I tapped into some of my demon's power, warming myself internally as Liam and I stepped out into the crisp January night. I didn't really need his arm around my shoulders, but I wasn't complaining. In fact, as we crossed the street back to Harvard Yard, I felt myself warming in other ways that had nothing to do with magic.

Unless hormones are magical.

This might work out after all. Once I managed to get out of my own way and stop being such a freakazoid about the future.

"Did I tell you?" Liam smiled down at me, snow crunching under our boots, a puff of white mist floating from his lips in the still night air. "Mom remarried."

There was a shocker. I hadn't heard from Sonja O'Dane since Liam used magic on her to make her leave us the hell alone. She'd been the reason Liam and I hadn't taken our relationship any further when I first decided he was the one for me. Her constant helicopter presence drove me crazy, to the point I just couldn't stand being with him anymore, knowing she was part of the deal.

But now, thanks to his spell, she'd lost her anxious need to be with him 24/7. And from the sounds of things, she'd made a life for herself. Somewhere else.

Away from me.

Wicked.

"That's nice." Wow, Syd. Way to show even a little bit of interest and genuine enthusiasm. But Liam didn't seem to notice my lack of caring.

"She's really happy," he said, one tartan patterned mitten rising to brush at his nose. "That's all I wanted for her."

That hit me where it hurt. Liam really was the sweetest, most adorable and big-hearted guy I'd ever met. I slid my arm around his waist and squeezed, even managing a smile. After all, I may have hated her guts for a lot of reasons—like almost getting her son killed on several occasions while being a general pain in my ass— but even I wasn't so jaded I couldn't share Lima's happiness for his mom.

And while I couldn't really muster happiness for Sonja, her allegiances did perk my interest. "Who did she marry?" Casual, Syd. Act casual.

Liam took me at my innocent worst.

"His name is Roger," he said. "A normal, amazingly enough. Owns a motorcycle repair shop in Maine."

Which meant she hadn't dipped her toes back into Unseelie business.

Awesome. My mood lightened immediately. Not only was she out of my life, she had a new one of her own and was staying out of mischief.

"You're a good boy," I said, winking.

I meant it as a joke. Just a sidebar ribbing, my specialty. So why did he frown suddenly and pull me to a stop?

"Syd." He gripped my shoulders in his mittened hands, pulling me closer to him. So close the puffiness of his jacket sighed against my navy wool pea coat, the distinct pressure of his physical need pressing to the zipper of my jeans. "I don't want to be a good boy."

Oh. My. Gulp. Swearword.

Blush much, Hayle? It was pretty clear from his pink cheeks—cold winter night or not—it took him a lot of courage to say so. His meaning was pretty obvious, even for someone as dense as me.

And how did I feel about it?

White flakes began to fall, fat, soft ones, as I stood there and tried to think of what to say to him, to decide what I wanted to do about the two of us. They settled in his lashes, on the bobble of his brown earflap hat. So. Freaking. Adorable.

How did I feel about it?

Growl.

He must have sensed the change in my mood, because he smiled shyly before bending over me. I reached up on my tiptoes, his earth magic rumbling through me. Shaylee embraced him whole-heartedly, though my demon turned her back, sulking in the corner. I knew what she wanted. Who. But Liam was here and I refused to let thoughts of Quaid—or my demon's longing for him—ruin this moment.

Liam's hot breath brushed over my lips, the scent of chocolate from his dessert washing over me as I slid both hands over the front of his jacket, fingers sliding between the snaps and under the puffy fabric to touch him through the thin material of his t-shirt.

I always expected his lips to burn me when he kissed me, the expectation built in from other encounters with a darker soul, but the cool depth of earth met my mouth instead. And then all memories of past embraces faded into nothing as I leaned in to Liam, one hand around the back of his neck, pulling him closer.

So strong, his arms, sweet his tongue. His cold nose pressed to my cheek, tiny snow kisses tingling on my skin as the fall came heavier. I ignored it, closing my eyes, grounding myself in his power as a deep, vibrating hum began at the soles of my feet and began to move upward.

Making me wonder what would happen when it

climbed a little further.

Something wet and hard hit the back of my head, knocking me forward. My teeth impacted Liam's with a clunk. We both jerked away, Liam holding his mouth where a small spot of red welled on his lower lip. I spun with a snarl at the sound of giggling, power gathering in a rush around me.

Jean Marc and Kristophe Dumont stood just past one of the large trees bordering the Yard. Kristophe's long, blonde hair was tied artfully back in a ponytail, his tailored long coat sweeping over the ground as he struck one of his model poses. But it was Jean Marc who brushed his hands together, evidence of who threw the offending snowball clear from his actions.

I guess they forgot I'd saved their damned asses, saved their whole coven from ruin when I rescued the Dumont family magic from the Brotherhood.

Gratitude went a long way with them.

"How adorable," Kristophe said. "*Oui, mon frère?*"

Jean Marc didn't say anything, just smiled at me, brow drawn low over his eyes.

It was only the fact we stood in the open, in the middle of the Yard, that kept their nasty little lives from total extermination. After all, I now had carte blanche from the High Council to act as I saw fit, didn't I? Yes, killing the Dumont brothers as horribly and painfully as possible was likely outside what the Council meant by "protecting all witches", but I considered it a public service.

Maybe the little children needed a reminder of just who they were prodding.

I grinned at Jean Marc. "You throw like a girl."

That hit the spot. Temper, temper, Dumont. His smirk faded immediately, eyes flaring with lavender fire. Now that he was second of his coven, chosen by his father Andre, I expected more of Jean Marc. Considering Andre's unusual position as the new leader of the Dumonts, the first male leader in witch history, I would have thought keeping a low profile would be on the menu. After all, my friend Mia crashed and burned from the loss of the family magic, but if Andre screwed up, I had no doubt the damaged girl would be right there, ready to pounce and demand yet again the Council return her power to her.

I guess either Andre didn't give a crap about what anyone thought or dear Johnny and Kris weren't following orders. More responsibility hadn't done wonders for either of them. They were still asshat bullies and always would be.

Kristophe was the worse of the two, if that was possible. The posing jerk had been pushing around other young witches all semester. I'd stepped in a time or two, but neither he nor his brother had the balls to confront me before now.

So what changed?

"Don't think you're unreachable, Hayle." Jean Marc crossed his arms over his chest, wide shoulders hulking behind his thick neck as he focused his power on me.

Made me laugh out loud.

"I'm right here, Johnny," I said, actually kind of enjoying myself. More so when his anger flared. Hoped he blew a gasket. Or better, used magic against me openly in the Yard.

His ass would be mine.

Liam went and ruined my plan for fun and revenge. "Why don't you two just leave her alone?"

Tell me he didn't step in front of me like I was some princess needing saving?

Facepalm.

While I adored Liam for his chivalry and kindness, he really had to understand the fact I didn't need him to stand up for me.

Kristophe took the bait, stalking toward us, swinging his ponytail like he was on a runway. Seriously?

"Mind your own business, Gatekeeper." Kristophe looked Liam up and down. Mostly up, since my friend had at least a head of height on him, not to mention width. "We don't converse with lesser beings."

What a jerk. But Liam was too smart to buy into Kristophe's—

One long arm pulled back, flew forward and, before I

could move, breathe, think, Kristophe was on the ground, blood flowing from his elegant European nose.

I stared up at Liam in total shock while Kristophe wailed in fury.

"How dare you?" The younger Dumont brother tried to scramble to his feet, but his coat was too long and the snow so thick under foot by then all he managed was a wet, flopping motion.

Like a beached sea monster failing in desperation for open water, all elegance lost in his four-limbed thrashing while Jean Marc cursed and slipped as he lunged for his brother, falling on his own sorry ass for his trouble.

A snort escaped me. Laughter broke from my lips. I bit them to try to stop the hilarity from rising, but I just couldn't make it stop.

Howling, grasping my aching ribs, I fell into hysterics as Jean Marc pushed himself to his feet and finally managed to jerk his brother up beside him. Liam tried to step in front of me again, but I shoved him aside, finally pulling myself under control, though the occasional giggle continued to escape.

"Keep your creature away from my brother." Jean Marc acted like Kristophe hadn't been asking for a punch in the face. Hell, I'd have done it long ago if I'd thought it would do any good.

"Whatever," I said, grinning so wide my cold cheeks tingled. "Keep your family away from mine."

Kristophe mopped at the blood on his face, still flowing despite the surge of magic I felt him release to staunch the flow. "At least one of your bodyguards didn't abandon you," he snarled. "Careful, *cher*, or this one will turn coward and run off like that wolf bitch of yours."

Jean Marc latched onto Kristophe and dragged him away, but the younger Dumont wasn't done.

"If you see her again," Kristophe said, fighting his brother as he slid and slipped over the accumulating snow, "tell her I miss our little lessons."

I let them go. Forced myself to breathe, all hilarity dead at the thought of Charlotte and what Kristophe and his sick mind could have done to her all the years the Dumonts owned her.

Shudder. One more word and I would have gone after him. One more jab and he'd be dead. I think Jean Marc must have known they'd pushed me about as far as they could, because he physically dragged Kristophe out of sight around one of the dorms.

I unwound slowly, heart hammering in rage and indignation for the weregirl, even as my old sadness came rushing back.

Why did she leave me?

I turned to Liam to find him scowling at the retreating brothers while cradling his right hand.

At least his aggressive stance and expression were enough to break my mood. In fact, a small smile tried to rise, even as I mentally rolled my eyes.

Tough guy, huh? Sigh.

Liam didn't protest when I took him by the sleeve and led him to his dorm, nor did he argue, now a little shame-faced, as I pushed him down on his bed and peeled away his mitten. Just my lightest touch to the swelling under his skin made him hiss in pain.

"Broken," I said, grinning at him as my giggles returned. "Idiot."

In his first show of defiance, he tried to pull his hand away, but I refused to let go. "It was time they knew who they were messing with."

I snorted, couldn't help it, as my power slid around his hand and knitted the bone. "My hero."

Liam's jaw clenched. Damn it, I'd pushed him too far, just as much as the Dumonts pushed me. Even my sweet, kind-hearted Sidhe friend was a guy first and foremost.

I let go of his hand and took his face between mine, forcing him to meet my eyes. He did, sullen anger at war with embarrassment written all over his face.

"Thank you," I said. Kissed him.

"You're welcome," he said. Kissed me back.

The rumble of our joining power came back, stronger than ever.

"You really are my hero," I said, the heat of our moment in the Yard returning. And in that instant, sitting there on his bed, looking into hazel eyes glittering with green sparks, I made a decision.

Liam. Okay then.

I slid into his lap and pushed him back, the sigh of his puffy coat between us. "Let me show you how much I appreciate being rescued."

chapter three

"Did you want more cream for your coffee?" Liam's big hand hovered over my steaming cup, already full to the brim thanks to his attentions. I felt my smile wavering despite my efforts to keep it in place.

I'd been smiling all morning, ever since I woke up next to him, warm and comfortable, the humming thrum of earth magic between us so powerful the bed vibrated ever so slightly. Wrapped in the scent of fresh turned soil and his amazing fabric softener, I opened my eyes to find him watching me with a soft, sweet expression on his face.

Only problem was, my smile felt more fake as time passed. Not because I had any regrets—not in the least. Though I had to admit I was a little shocked to find out I was the only one with experience. Still, Liam was attentive and gentle when he needed to be and more than eager when I asked for more.

It was a long, fun night. One I was more than happy to repeat.

At least, that's what I told myself as he leaned in and kissed me when I woke, the morning sun shining on his blonde hair, red cast glowing softly in the light.

"I love you," he whispered.

Choke. "I love you, too." Oh. My. Swearword. Did I really hesitate?

He didn't take it as an issue, fingers stroking over the bare skin of my shoulder before sliding into my hair. "I know you have to marry soon," he said, voice soft, deep, each word thudding inside my heart, "and I want you to marry me."

Gasp, splutter. EEK.

I'd just managed to push the future out of my head and he brought it crashing back around me. Perfect.

I sat up abruptly, pulling away from him, still smiling. "Thanks," I said, breathless as I slid from his bed and fought panic as I flailed around for my clothes.

Thanks? Holy hell, Syd. Really?

I had to get a grip.

Liam's face fell, as he watched me thrash around like an idiot for a minute.

"Syd," he said.

I froze, turned with my underwear in hand, bra half on. Looked into the deer in the headlights that were his sad eyes.

"I didn't mean today," he said.

Breathe.

Just. Freaking. Breathe.

I sank to the edge of the bed, forcing out a deep breath, knees shaking, hands shaking, all of me one big shake-shake-shake.

Liam's hand settled on my thigh as he slid across to me, pressing his cheek to my shoulder, hair tickling my back.

"Are you okay?"

I swallowed hard, sagged. "I'm sorry," I said, tears welling in my eyes, prickling the back of my throat. "I didn't mean to wig out. It's just…"

"I get it." Liam pulled away, shifted again until he sat beside me, the top sheet draped modestly across his lap. "I shouldn't have pushed you like that."

I turned and hugged him, the underwire of my bra poking me as it swung sideways, but I didn't care. He felt solid, real. Comfortable.

So why was I so freaked out?

"Let's go to breakfast." He slid on his boxers, stood and offered me the underwear I'd dropped. So weird seeing my pink hot lips undies hanging from his fingers.

It took a lot not to snatch them back.

Liam didn't say much while we dressed, though he was so gently attentive I wanted to scream. Why did it bother me he loaded his toothbrush for me to use? Or held my coat for me to put on? Opened the door, all gallant. Offered his arm as we entered the Yard.

My head buzzed, smile cemented on my face as I fought to understand what the hell was wrong with me. I loved Liam, didn't I? Of course I did. And we were clearly physically compatible if last night was any indication. So why was I gritting my teeth as he hovered close, practically cutting my pancakes for me?

Oh. My. Swearword.

Not practically. Did he really just butter my freaking toast?

Breathe. Remember breathing. It's necessary.

"You're so amazing." Liam leaned in, pressed his lips to my temple while my heart tightened, my chest compressing the life out of me. "I had no idea it could be so incredible between us."

I looked up into his eyes, ready to push him away and froze.

Dead in my tracks.

Because I recognized the look on his face. The same one I'd seen in the mirror the morning after I'd first slept with Quaid.

Adoration. Infatuation. Love.

Reality check. The way I was feeling didn't match, not even a little. Was this how Quaid felt about me that same morning? Was I now somehow going to do to Liam what

Quaid did to me?

Gram's face flashed in my mind, her scowl, her words. How Liam was weak, not strong enough for me. And in that moment, staring into his dreamy, adoring eyes, I believed her.

Then snapped the hell out of it.

No way was I going to break his heart like Quaid broke mine. No. Way.

I reached up and touched his cheek with my fingertips. "I love you, too," I said, meant it. Put everything I had into it. "But I can butter my own damned toast."

Liam laughed. Nodded. Backed off.

Phew.

I let my rock-hard smile collapse, shuddered gently. Got a freaking grip.

The moment I unclenched, I immediately felt better. I was not Quaid. I would not make Liam's first time a mess of grief and heartbreak. Whether I married my Sidhe boyfriend or not, he would only ever know I loved him.

Breakfast over, we crossed back to the Yard, heading for his dorm. I really needed—wanted—to go home and be alone for a few hours, but the pleading look on his face told me he was expecting something else. We both grabbed a quick wash in his shower and, I have to admit, his height made things interesting, not to mention how fun water could make our little party. The only frustrating part was the fact he couldn't seem to tolerate the temperature I loved, so despite the giggling and sighing part of our joint shower, I left his bathroom feeling vaguely cheated.

When we came up for air hours later, the late afternoon sun leaving a rim of red on the horizon, I took him to my room with me, grateful to be back in my own space.

When Liam tried to follow me into the shower, I gently pressed my hand to his chest and gave him a little shove before closing the bathroom door behind me. Maybe I should have let him join me, but frankly, I was tired, craving heat after being out in the cold. And a girl just needed some privacy now and then.

Steam poured out of the stall as I cranked up the temperature, stepping in with a sigh of happiness. I let it cascade over me for a solid minute before getting down to business.

I was part way through shaving my left leg when Sunny's voice spoke in my mind.

Syd.

A little meep escaped my lips, followed by a hiss of pain as the razor sliced through my skin, a thin line of red instantly running from my shin. I healed it as I stood up, reached back to the queen of the Wilhelm clan even as I winced and blocked my location from her mind.

Hi, Sunny. I set the razor aside, hugging myself under

the stream of hot water, resisting the urge to grab a towel and feeling very awkward about the whole situation.

Did I get you at a bad time? No humor in her voice, just mild curiosity.

What's up? Not going there.

I was wondering if you were coming to visit this evening. I felt her walking, caught flashes of the stone halls of the Austrian castle she called home, felt the brush of Uncle Frank's mind next to hers.

Panicked at his touch, I reached for the shower curtain, wrapping it tightly around me though I knew neither of them could see where I was.

Didn't matter. Ew. Just ew.

Um… my mind went to Liam. *Not sure.*

Is everything all right? Sunny's focus tightened. *Are you in trouble?*

No. I sighed. *Just… Liam's here.*

Sunny's startled surge turned to wicked understanding in a flash.

I see. Sorry to interrupt. Why did she have to sound so sultry just then?

Not here, *here.* I felt my skin heat from the inside, forget the hot water pouring over me. *Just piss off.*

Sunny's laughter actually made me grin.

We'll talk later, she sent.

I have no idea what prompted me to pull her mind back to mine, but for some reason, talking to Sunny made me think of Charlotte. And what Kristophe said the night before.

Can you do me a favor? I bit my lower lip, knowing I was crossing a line, but unable to help myself any longer. I had to know if the weregirl was all right.

Anything, you know that. Sunny's mind hugged me.

I need to find Charlotte. She'd kill me for not minding my own business. *But I don't want her to know I'm looking.* Yeah, like anyone poking around asking about her wouldn't lead back to me.

And my vampires may be able to find her unobtrusively. Sunny's forward motion halted. I caught a glimpse of her throne room, the rustling sound of her dress as she sat. *Consider it done.*

I know you're not exactly friends. Werewolves and vampires did not get along.

While our two races may not be allies, Sunny sent, *that fact is only thanks to the sorcery which created them. Our spirit magic and their sorcerous core repel each other like oil and water.*

Well now. I'd never made that connection before.

It makes complete sense, my vampire said in her dry, cool voice. *I'm surprised you never considered it.*

Smartass alter ego.

I've grown very fond of Charlotte, Sunny sent. *And I, too, have wondered how she's doing. I'll be in touch if I find out anything.*

Thanks. Relief washed over me, the wave so powerful

I actually felt a little weak. I had no idea my worry for the weregirl was affecting me so much until the weight of it lifted.

Love you, Sunny sent. Giggled. *Have fun with Liam.*

Groan.

I'd never hear the end of it, now.

The wet fabric curtain peeled from my skin as I let it go, cranking the water hotter, letting it fall over me as I relaxed into the heat. Pride or no pride, Charlotte was my friend and, in many ways, family. I'd done my best to keep from interfering in her life, but the least she could have done was let me know, at some point, she was okay.

Six months was as long as I could take. Like it or not, Charlotte had to understand she couldn't just cut off the people who loved her and not expect us to go looking for her.

CHAPTER FOUR

My initial knee-jerk, irritated reaction to Liam's star-struck lover boy routine faded as the weekend passed. In fact, by the time I languidly rose from his bed late Sunday afternoon, the smile I found on my face, reflected back to me from his bathroom mirror, was real and rather comical.

I'd never been one to accept being catered to. In fact, I was usually the one taking matters into my own hands. But having Liam wait on me hand and foot was becoming rather addictive.

His shower was smaller than mine, his shampoo all wrong for my hair, but whatever. I'd adapt. And make sure I stocked his bathroom with my stuff in the future. For now, I enjoyed more steam, more hot water, hugging myself with happiness and wondering what all my earlier fuss was about.

This could really go somewhere after all. It really could. I pictured myself walking down the aisle, looking up through demurely fluttering lashes, meeting chocolate eyes—

Damn it.

I turned the water off, wrapping myself in the large, plush bath sheet Liam left out for me. Why was I thinking about Quaid when Liam slept in the next room? After I spent the whole weekend engrossed in Liam, physically as well as emotionally?

I leaned against the counter, hugging the towel to me as I admitted how much it hurt I hadn't heard much from tall, dark and deliciously jerkish. He'd been keeping his distance since summer, focused, I could only guess, on his last year of training with the Enforcer order.

Not that I blamed him. No matter how I felt, no matter the fact my demon pined and growled at me until Shaylee wouldn't talk to her anymore, Quaid was lost to me, and I really, really had to get over him.

Was doing a smashing job. Just smashing.

Ack.

I peeked out the bathroom door, Liam's sweet, sleeping face turned toward me, bare chest rising and falling slowly as he breathed, one arm flung out over the place I'd left. Liam loved me so much, would do anything for me. He could be the one.

At least until he grew old and died while I stayed young.

Yeah, way to crush the moment underfoot and leave a smear of hurt behind, Hayle.

I squeezed water from my hair, hating the scowl on my face, my eyes flaring with blue fire as I caught my reflection again. I would not make Liam second best to a guy who chose his career over being with me. Time to choose to be happy with the Sidhe Gatekeeper. To pick kind and sweet over sarcastic and moody.

Considering I was more the latter than the former, we'd be a fit, wouldn't we? I could grow to like being taken care of. And there would be no jealousy from Liam I was more powerful than him.

Not like with Quaid.

I very firmly drew a box around every single feeling I had for my first love and sealed it with as much power as I could before leaving the bathroom. I sank to the side of the bed, held my long, wet hair out of the way, bending to brush my lips over Liam's. He reacted immediately, arms rising to pull me to him, eyes cracking open, wide mouth smiling. I snuggled against his chest, my damp towel still warm from the heat of the water I'd used. He'd been more than willing to turn up the heat, but we'd figured out very quickly his skin couldn't handle the temperatures I loved and I wondered how much of my craving for super-heated showers had to do with my demon.

"Love you," he mumbled.

"Love you, too," I said. Felt and heard my stomach rumble. "Hungry?"

Liam's smile made me wish I didn't need dinner just yet.

It was nice to hold his hand, to swing my arm in time with his. No more freak outs, not while I settled into his rhythm. Funny how it only took a couple of days for this to feel like it had always been between us.

Nice.

My little bubble of happy didn't protect me from the outside world, though. Not while a familiar figure approached, one arm raised. I tensed immediately as Mia crossed the snowy Yard to join us. The last time I'd seen her, she accused me of interfering with her coven, tried to have me burned for the loss of her family magic. I felt terrible for her, guilty the very same magic she'd lost to the Brotherhood chose to go to Andre Dumont instead of home to her. But I knew it was her weakness that made the theft possible in the first place.

So much guilt around my old friend. Her mother did her no favors blocking her magic when she was a baby. Clare Dumont fled her family and her crazy mother, Odette, for a chance to give Mia and Quaid normal lives. But the now-dead leader of the Dumont family hadn't been willing to let things lie. Knowing she could only protect one of her children, she chose the infant Mia over one-year-old Quaid, perhaps sensing her daughter didn't have the strength of her son.

Regardless, I couldn't help but think Clare made the wrong choice. Being cut off from her magic caused a crack in Mia's psyche, which had only grown over the years as she struggled to understand what she was missing. Sure, it could have gone either way, especially if Mia was a little more stable. Considering Gram's own fight with her loss of magic had only made her stronger, in my opinion. Mia's story could have ended differently if she'd had support.

But my grandmother was powerful to begin with, hardheaded and stubborn. Not to mention the fact she lost her magic as an adult woman.

Mia wasn't so lucky—or so grounded. It still showed on her face as she smiled at me, eyes a little wild, cheeks sunken. She looked like she'd dropped twenty pounds, and not in a good way. Gaunt, pale skin parched, her black Goth makeup did nothing to improve her appearance.

But her smile shook me far more deeply than her looks. The way she reached for my free hand, acted like there had never been darkness between us as her cold lips pressed to my cheek.

"Syd!" Mia leaned away, meager power reaching for mine and, on impulse, I reached back. She ignored Liam like he wasn't even there. Rude. Very rude. But he took her attitude in stride and, with a slow nod, backed off and allowed her to take my attention.

While I struggled to accept her arrogance, knowing, even as I did, it was grounded in an underground self-esteem issue tied to a severe lack of confidence, he immediately understood what she needed and acted without ego.

Yeah, he'd do.

"It's so lovely to run into you." Mia's hair, the only healthy looking part of her, caught the gloss of the white lights bordering the Yard.

Um, okay. Not like she didn't know where to find me all along.

"Mia." I did my best to grasp some balance. She was so mercurial, I wondered if an explosion waited behind her clear blue eyes.

"I've been wanting to talk to you for so long." Her shoulders slumped, smile fading, though she seemed less ready to snap and more introspective, so I took it as a good thing. "The way I treated you, how I acted when all you did was try to help me and my family." She shook her head, hair swinging, a thread catching at the corner of her mouth. "Inexcusable."

"I'm so sorry, too." Guilt gushed out of me as I hugged her, relief curling free from months of old hurt. "I've been worried about you."

Mia smiled again as I released her. "That's sweet. But

I'm doing okay." She turned and gestured. Only then did I notice a pair of young witches hovering behind her. "I've started my own family."

Her attempt at perky fell flat, but I wasn't going to call her on it. And from the feel of the pair, they were even weaker than Mia. Made me sad, but at least she was trying, right?

Right?

She glanced around as though we were being observed before bending her head, voice dropping in volume and timber. "I wanted to tell you that thanks to you, I've seen the light."

All of her crazy came back in a rush. Not in her face or her bearing. But in that moment, with those words and the ones following, I understood she was not only still broken, the pieces left of her were now starting to fracture as well. "I've found the true path of magic." She shivered, eyes widening. "There is so much to learn, Syd." Mia's hand grasped mine again, intensity in her face, a reverence and fanaticism reminding me of the Chosen of the Light. But at least that deranged group had a powerful leader at one point, someone to keep them safe. While I didn't agree with Demetrius Strong's old ways, I understood his methods. Mia just didn't have the wherewithal to support others, let alone herself.

She shivered in delight, lips pursing in a pert smile. "There is so much power to be had." One sharp nod ended her little episode into heretic. "When the time comes, of all people, I'll be happy to share my knowledge with you."

"Thanks," I said. There wasn't much else to say to crazy.

Mia hugged me again. Smiled brightly. "You're welcome."

Turned and left without another word, her sad little pair of followers trailing after her.

"What the hell was that?" Liam's arm went around my shoulders, pulling me against him.

"I have no idea." Yes, I could have invaded Mia's mind and found out. But honestly, she wasn't a threat to me, to anyone, not anymore.

Let her have her delusions if they made her life easier. The elements knew she earned some peace.

Liam hugged me, warm breath in my ear even through my hat. "It's not your fault."

"I know." I hugged him back. Kissed him. "Thank you."

But as we moved on, the beckoning lights of Memorial Hall calling us to dinner, I couldn't help but wonder if there was more I could have done for Mia.

CHAPTER FIVE

Dinner was quiet, the girls keeping their distance, though I'd tried a couple of times to have them join us. But their giggling and winks were enough to tell me they had no intention of separating Liam and I just yet.

I knew once the weekend was officially over they'd pile on top of me for deets.

I felt Shenka return, her connection to the family magic alerting me as she arrived back at Harvard. For a moment, I sensed her tie to Enforcer magic, and I kicked myself a little. Of course she'd need help to get home. Without my ability to ride the veil between our plane and Demonicon as her means of travel, I'd left Shenka to fend for herself.

She must have felt my guilt, because she immediately reached for me.

If you're thinking what I know you're thinking, you're being silly. Her mental tone sounded firm, but loving. *I managed just fine, thank you. Besides, I had a cute ride.*

Gulp. Heart clench. Chocolate and leather and hot magic—

No, she sent, mind hugging mine gently and a little sadly. *Not him. I'd never do that to you.*

Of course she wouldn't. But my reaction to the possibility set me off in a way I wasn't expecting. Turned out, the box of Quaid I'd sequestered with magic wasn't working after all.

Because, yeah. That would be too easy.

I hugged her back, hiding my churning emotions from her. *I'll see you soon.*

She let me go as I turned to Liam, my buzz of happiness now long gone. "Shenka's back."

He seemed to collapse in on himself a little. Did he sense he'd lost me? And had he? His smile was as sweet as ever. "I guess our weekend is over."

I hugged him, his cold cheek pressed to mine even as I struggled with what to say, how to act all of a sudden. The ease of our being felt lost and I didn't know how to bring it back.

"I'll see you in the morning." His lips demanded I stay with him, but I parted from him after only a moment. I stood in the Yard, hands in my pockets as Liam turned and left me there, looking back over his shoulder and waving twice before disappearing into his dorm.

Sigh.

I had to figure this Quaid thing out or I'd never get married.

My boots made thudding sounds as I trudged through the snow, shoulders hiking up around my ears, shivering at the sudden cold enveloping me. My demon hated winter and I was inclined to agree with her.

I find it refreshing, my vampire sent.

Both Shaylee and my demon snarled at her.

The warm interior of Hollis Hall welcomed me as I entered, climbed the stairs. My feet slowed as I neared my door. Sudden reluctance pulled on me. Why was I so hesitant to see Shenka, to tell her the inevitable happened? It wasn't like she didn't know what Liam's weekend solitude was all about.

Still, as I reached for the doorknob, I felt discomfort and confusion ramp up. The feeling things weren't quite right, the spell Liam and I wove around each other the last two days wasn't real, couldn't—shouldn't—last.

I was going to girlfriend hell.

Shenka sat on her bed, smiling as I came inside, her magic hugging me even as she rose and came to do so physically. I hugged her back, our family magic linking us together.

"So," she said, deep brown eyes sparkling as she

pulled away. "How was your weekend?"

Blush. Ing.

She pulled me down on the bed with her and, embarrassed, but oddly giggly, I shed my coat and gloves and told her everything. Well, not everything. But enough she squealed and hugged me before hesitating.

"I adore Liam," Shenka said. "He's lovely."

"But." I stood up, went to my side of the room, stared out the window over my bed into the cold January night. Hated how my heart clenched around Quaid and wouldn't let go.

I heard the rustle of fabric as she moved. "When he asked me what to do, I encouraged him to suggest this weekend."

My grin widened as I turned to face her. "Didn't see that coming."

She snorted. "Hush, you." Her hands settled in her lap as she shrugged, on foot bobbing over the edge of the bed in agitation. "I was hoping you would either see the light about him, or…"

"See the light." I sank onto my own bed. "Pick him or scratch him from the list."

She nodded. "And?"

And.

"Whatever choice you make," Shenka said, "you know I'm behind you. I always will be."

I chewed my thumbnail. Not everyone felt the same

way. "How's Gram?"

Shenka's smile faded before returning. I knew her tells already, the signs when she was trying to hide something from me. "She's fine."

Um-hum.

"Honestly, she's still in her room most of the time." Shenka tossed her hands, both landing with soft thuds in her lap. "I'm worried about her, Syd."

That made two of us. Gram and I had shared a unique connection ever since I was a baby, thanks to the power she embedded in me to protect her magic from the Purity family when they attacked. Because I carried it for so long, it was as though we shared part of a soul. There were times when Gram's eavesdropping irritated me and others when I couldn't have imagined making it through my life without her.

But now that she'd lost most of her magic to Ameline, our connection was so weak I barely felt her. And thanks to her stubborn melancholy over the whole thing, she refused to let me in anymore.

More than anything, without Gram, I felt like I'd lost part of myself and didn't know how to get it back.

Not true. I had to kill Ameline. That would solve everything.

Stupid maji prophecy keeping the bitch alive. It could just bite me.

"I can't tell if she's getting stronger." Shenka tapped a

beat out on her thigh with her fingertips. "But I don't think she is. Though Lula Kennecott was there for a visit and to give her a checkup."

I brightened a little at that. The sister half of the Kennecott twins was one-half of an amazing healer team. I adored both she and her brother, Phon, and knew Gram was in good hands.

"How did she take that?" I could just imagine my grandmother's reaction to being poked and prodded magically, regardless Lula's smooth and gentle temperament.

Shenka laughed. "You can guess. But Lula is amazing with her. After Ethpeal got through griping and fighting with Sassafras over what was and wasn't good for her, she finally relented and let Lula do her work."

I could so picture it. Made me sad knowing I missed so much. I wished I could split myself into pieces and not ever miss a thing...

Then again, I'd had my other parts stripped from me before, and I really preferred keeping us intact.

"Oh, and Talee's son, Todd, had a bit of an altercation with the Mitchell's boy. A fight over who was a real coven member." Shenka chuckled. "A few fists were thrown, and Hiller lost a tooth that was loose anyway."

Yikes. How did she handle this stuff? I would have shaken the two of them and knocked their heads together.

"I'm so lucky to have you," I said, love and more guilt welling inside me. "I should have been home with you this weekend."

Shenka's frown had nothing to do with anger as she rose and came to my side, sitting next to me, taking my hand.

"I've told you before," she said. "This is my job. And I love it, Syd." Her beaming smile was so genuine I smiled back, my soul uncurling from regret. "Thank you so much for asking me. Yes, I was second for my family, with Tallah. But they knew me as their coven leader's sister." Her perfect, white teeth flashed as she shook her head, lips in a wry twist. "I didn't really get the chance to be the one they came to. But with our family," she bloomed again, a dark rose framed by long, silky black hair, "I'm finally able to be the witch, the leader, I wanted to be." She jabbed me gently with one elbow. "While you take on the big, nasty stuff. It's a win-win."

I hugged her hard, throat tight. "You're awesome."

She laughed in my ear. "Syd," she whispered, "the feeling is so mutual."

We smiled at each other, both tearing up before Shenka laughed again and gave me a little shove.

"No crying," she said.

Snort. Yeah, I was really good at the no crying thing.

Syd. Sunny's mental voice broke through as I sobered,

linking Shenka to the conversation immediately.

Hey. I raised my eyebrows at Shenka who cocked her head in curiosity.

Hello, Sunny, she sent to the vampire queen.

Shenka, darling. Sunny's spirit power embraced us both. *I'm happy you're with Syd. I have news about Charlotte.*

Instant perk. Shenka's soft gasp came in conjunction with the tightening of her hands in mine.

Is she okay?

Where is she?

Shenka and I stumbled over each other as Sunny went on.

The feeling from the vampire queen wasn't positive.

I don't know, she sent. *Not in detail. But what I've found out worries me.*

I was on my feet, my second beside me, already reaching for my coat.

I'll be right there.

Because, no matter my boy troubles, my crazy life, I would drop everything in a heartbeat.

This was Charlotte we were talking about.

chapter six

Shenka and I stepped out of the veil in the Wilhelm throne room. Sunny approached us immediately, Uncle Frank behind her. I hugged the stunning, blonde queen, feeling the warmth of her body, telling me she'd fed not too long ago. It used to bother me, thinking about how vampires survived, though only peripheral bother. But now I carried the vampire essence inside me, had almost died from being drained of my blood and left a withered mummy, I had a totally different perspective.

Uncle Frank's arms pulled me in, his broad chest just how I remembered it. Every time he hugged me, I felt like I was a little girl all over again, with my tall, handsome uncle looking out for me.

Just because he was a vampire didn't mean he couldn't be the best uncle ever.

Had my vote.

"I don't know how much time we have," Sunny said, taking my hand and leading me toward the back of the throne room. I looked up at the stained glass window, a beautiful, round piece of art depicting Sunny and Uncle Frank, smiling in tinted silicate. The previous one, a more deathly scene, but stunning nonetheless, had been shattered last summer when I freed the Wilhelm Blood Clan from the sorcerer's taint. Nice to see they'd gotten around to replacing it with something happier.

"Applegate promised me she'd stay out of things, but I'm not sure she really meant it." Sunny's chin tilted to the right where a small group of vampires waited, her court always assembled, it seemed. Piotr Wilhelm, my biggest vampire fan aside from Celeste and Pannera Sthol, glared at me before turning and leaving the throne room.

"You do know he's snitching on us, right?" I had no doubt in my mind the handsome, if arrogant and totally misguided, vampire still blamed me for the death of his beloved queen, Yvette. Like it was my fault Batsheva Moromond turned her power-stealing ways from witches to vampires after almost destroying the North American High Council. Or that Yvette hadn't been strong enough to stand against the Brotherhood and Batsheva.

That, I would never feel guilt over.

Sunny sat gracefully on a low divan, her skirts whispering around her. Though she and Uncle Frank had mostly abandoned the vampire's tradition of wearing elaborate court attire, she still dressed more formally than her favorite suits and jeans. I took a seat next to her, Shenka joining Uncle Frank on a matching bench just opposite, the four of us tucked behind the throne dais for a little privacy.

I shuddered at the cold, amping up my demon's power to push back the chill of the air in the old castle. Sunny hissed softly at my personal temperature when she gripped my hand, though she didn't pull away.

"Sorry," she said with a kind smile. "You always suffer the cold here."

"You're just lucky you don't feel it." I shivered, forcing my jaw to relax so my teeth wouldn't chatter. A waft of steam rose from my breath as my demon stepped up the heat. "So why don't you boot Piotr's ass if he's making trouble?"

And trouble was coming, yes indeed. Always did, in the form of Margaret Applegate. No matter what I did, how I shielded, how much I pushed down my power, within ten minutes of arriving at Castle Wilhelm, I was invariably confronted with the arrogant and angry form of European Council Leader and her posse of grim-faced Enforcers. I noticed her Enforcer leader never joined her and often wondered where was Elliot Pearson. The jovial Irish witch at least kind of liked me, though I was positive Applegate's animosity had less to do with personal reasons and more with the Brotherhood's attempt to take her over.

Didn't make me like her any more, though.

Sunny shrugged, pulling away. "You asked about Charlotte."

Ah. Oops. I guess I did step over the line. I'd never accept Sunny telling me what to do with my coven, so fair enough.

"I did," I said. "Thank you for looking into it for me."

She accepted my focus as my apology as much as I did her redirect as a rebuke. Loved her for her class.

"I want you to meet someone." Sunny looked up, gestured. I glanced over Shenka's shoulder, saw a slim, pretty girl emerge from the shadows. No, not a girl. A vampire, her light brown hair rippling with streaks of gold, bright eyes almost the same color. She dipped a bobbing curtsy to me, slender body wrapped in a dark cloak.

"Hi," I said. Looked at Sunny.

"This is Isabelle," the vampire queen said. "She has the news you asked for."

The young woman—vampire—bobbed again, small hands gripped tight before her. "Coven Leader," she said in a refined voice. "When my queen asked for information about the werewolves, I immediately contacted a friend in the Ukraine."

Charlotte's old stomping grounds. That made sense.

I nodded for her to go on.

"I don't know how much you know about werewolves, Coven Leader?"

"Educate me." Yeah, really didn't know much at all. I'd asked a few questions of Charlotte, but she never answered. And though a few of her werewolf friends hung around a bit after she first bonded to me, they left shortly after Mom took over as Council Leader.

A little anger stirred inside me. Aimed at Charlotte. Stubborn, tight-lipped, bratski—

Isabelle shed her robe in a fluid motion, revealing jeans and a black turtleneck sweater. I did a bit of a double take, she seemed so ordinary. Well, except for her beauty, how pale her skin was.

The fact she was undead.

Yeah. Ordinary.

"I was born in the Ukraine," Isabelle said. I could hear the hint of her accent despite her polished tone, the same accent Charlotte struggled with when the weregirl grew emotional. "My family was tied to the faction who created the werewolves so long ago."

"Sorcerers?" I looked at Sunny then back at the vampire girl. "Are you saying you were a sorcerer before you were turned?"

"My father was," Isabelle said. "But my mother was normal. My brothers had power, but my sisters and I were latent. It is often this way with sorcery. The magic falls to one gender or the other in the bloodline."

Another thing I didn't know. Educate me, no kidding.

"So your family was—or is—Brotherhood." I tried not to judge her, but damn it, I'd almost had it up to my aching eyeballs with Liander Belaisle and his crew.

Isabelle shook her head, spiraled waves moving in ripples around her shoulders. "Not at all," she said. "Nor were they Steam Union."

Right. The "good" sorcerers. I had as yet to believe that was possible, though Demetrius Strong had proven a wonderful ally after shaking free of the Brotherhood, and he had originally been part of the mysterious Steam Union at one point. At least, until he lost his marbles.

"The sorcerers who created the werewolves are a small sect," Isabelle said. Was her voice shaking all of a sudden? "Led by a powerful family. They resisted both the Brotherhood and the Steam Union for centuries, keeping to themselves. It was their goal to become Creators." She paused. "To out-create the maji."

Interesting. "I take it they failed." Didn't think my voice could come out any drier without me choking on it.

"They did." A ghost of a smile widened her rosy lips. "The werewolves might be fast healing and very strong, but they lack their own magic. Like vampires, they *are* magic. But we have access to ours, can use it to our advantage. Werewolves' only ability is their shape shifting and extra strength."

"Which they cannot always control." Sunny patted my knee as she spoke before gesturing for Isabelle to continue.

"The sect was known as the *чорні душі*, the Black Souls, and, as a way to protect themselves from others, they formed an alliance with the Russian royal family. The earliest Czars always had werewolves as bodyguards and sorcerers as advisors." Isabelle shifted a little on her bench. "You've heard of Grigori Rasputin?"

"He was a sorcerer?" My history lessons came back, a vague memory of a hairy guy women supposedly went nutso over, murdered by the last Czar, Nicholas II, for sleeping with the queen or something.

"He was," she said. "And, at that time, he was the *чорні душі* leader. It was his desire to end the reign of Nicholas II, but was murdered before he could bring his plan to fruition." She shivered. "He was a terrible man, but he held sway over the sect and his death marked the turning point where the Black Souls turned against the Imperial family and plotted their removal." She wrinkled her nose. "And Yure Danko took his place."

Why was I not surprised some sorcerers had something to do with world-changing events?

"It was he who conspired to incite the revolution and it was the Black Souls who murdered the last of the Russian Imperial Romanovs." Isabelle's chin dropped, a soft sigh escaping her. "My family, Coven Leader. I worked as a governess for their daughter, Anastasia. All of us did, those without power but connected by blood to the Black Souls. When the Romanovs were killed, when my family betrayed those I loved, I fled the country."

And somehow became a vampire. I was so wrapped up in her story I wanted to ask more. But this was supposed to be about Charlotte.

Isabelle must have realized it at the same moment, because she shook herself a little. "The werewolves were bonded to the Imperial family, but because their creators were the murderers, there was nothing the wolf folk could do. Once a proud and mighty fighting force, forced to watch their bonded die, the werewolves descended into despair."

I flinched, remembering Charlotte's death. "Assholes," I said.

"Agreed," Isabelle said. "This was a huge blow to their *сан*." I'd heard that word before. Charlotte told me about it when she refused to leave me even though her life was in mortal danger at the time I was held by the vampire queens. Isabelle wrinkled her nose. "The closest I can come to in translation is 'blood honor'. The werewolves stood on their word, were known to be faithful and courageous to the very end. But once their souls were broken, they never recovered." Another pause. "Well, most of them."

Whatever that meant. I didn't get a chance to ask.

"And now?" Shenka's voice startled me. I'd forgotten she was there.

"Now," Isabelle said, "they are a pack of bullies, used by the Black Souls sect, forced to do their bidding, reduced to thugs and animals." Anger ran under her voice, words shuddering with it. "The sorcerers use them to control the mafia."

Um, what?

Isabelle's lips twisted as she smiled a little. "Yes," she said. "I see your surprise. But it is the *чорні душі* which created and control the majority of organized crime in Europe."

So the Brotherhood weren't the only ones taking on normals as targets.

Sorcerers sucked.

"The werewolves remain low in numbers, partly because of a very strict breeding program." Like they really were animals. That core of anger fanned into smoking coals at the thought of Charlotte being treated like cattle. "And all but one family has succumbed to the pressure of the sect, owned by them but refusing to bow to their rule."

Oh *hell* yeah. "Let me guess," I said. "Charlotte's family." Because, that would be just like her, wouldn't it?

Isabelle nodded, but sadly. "It is true," she said. "But their numbers are small, and dwindle further every generation. If Charlotte can't be saved, it is possible her loss could finally mean the end to the werewolf royal family."

Wait. Saved?

Hang on. Royal family?

Holy.

CHAPTER SEVEN

I gaped a minute, trying to breathe, to react, something. Anything.

Shenka finally beat me to it.

"Are you saying Charlotte is a princess?" I met her equally shocked eyes as Isabelle frowned and looked back and forth between us.

"You didn't know?" The young vampire shrugged. "I suppose it makes sense. Honor would keep her from doing anything to jeopardize your bond. And I'm certain, from what I've heard of you," she smiled again, just a little, "had you known of the plight of her people, you would have acted to help them."

Was that hope in her voice? If so, what tie did Isabelle have to the werewolves beyond her family's past? Because no way did she have a reaction like that to ancient history.

Had to be a guy involved.

Yup, yup.

"The Moreau family is led by Oleksander, Charlotte's grandfather." Isabelle's previously still hands wrung together suddenly. "From what I've been able to discover, Charlotte returned home, only to be imprisoned by the Black Souls and their leader, the Czar." She shook her hands out before resting them in her lap again. "He thinks himself the ruler of everything, has adopted the title now despised by the werewolves. But Yure Danko is not to be treated lightly. Because of his control of most of the organized crime in this part of the world, he commands forces of normals as well as the werewolves and his own small sect of sorcerers."

He couldn't be that scary. I was maji. Then again… the Brotherhood left him alone. "Why hasn't Belaisle gone after him?" Not like the Brotherhood leader to let someone get the better of him.

Isabelle's shoulders twitched. "I told you," she said. "He is not to be handled lightly."

Well, regardless who this dude thought he was, if he was holding my friend hostage, he was about to find out what kind of hurt I could put on him. Sorcerer or not, crime boss or not, if one hair on Charlotte's head was out of place, I'd find a very slow and painful way to make him see just how unhappy I was with his contribution to her hurt.

Right before I tore his little sect to pieces.

Wouldn't you know, the moment I surged to my feet to go to Charlotte's rescue, even if I had to drag Isabelle along with me to show me where to find this Czar and his nasty little hidey hole, the air in the throne room shuddered before erupting in puffs of blue flame.

Margaret Applegate flashed into view, a dozen black-robed Enforcers behind her. Seeing her made my heart sink to the tips of my boots even as I strode into the main throne room to face her.

"Coven Leader," she grated through clenched teeth. "You're in Europe again. Without permission."

"Council Leader," I snarled even as my chest tightened as I realized she now had me cornered. "I'm in my blood clan's territory. As you very well know."

"As I am forced to inform you," Sunny said, white power flaring around her as she rose into the air, coming to hover before the still floating Applegate, "every single time Sydlynn comes to visit." I felt bodies behind me, knew Shenka and Uncle Frank must have followed.

Applegate ignored the vampire queen, still focused on me. Her anger flared raw and full of blackness. How could her people not see what held her in thrall? The temptation to free her was so powerful I almost acted.

Almost.

If you are wrong, my vampire sent, casual but chilling, *if she is merely insane and not under their control, you will be arrested and burned at the stake. And if she is under their control and you fail, you will suffer the same result. And Sunny will not be able to save you. Nor will your mother. You will start a war between territories. Are you prepared for that?*

Damn it. I hated when she was right.

"Do you have intent to leave this castle?" Applegate's eyes flickered sideways, falling on Piotr. How subtle. I was going to kill him.

But I had no choice, did I? If he knew who I was looking for—and I had no doubt he did—he also likely knew what Isabelle told me. Or, at least, enough of the history to piece it together. I could just barge my way around Europe. Swoop in, if I could pinpoint Charlotte's location, and scoop her out of danger. But my vampire essence was right. The state Applegate was in, I was on the brink of starting a war I knew the Brotherhood would love to finish.

Because whether I had absolute proof or not, I knew she was under their control.

"One of my people is missing." Yeah, sure, Syd. Appealing to Applegate's softer, gentler bitch would really get me what I wanted. "She's being held against her will." Maybe. If Isabelle was right. "I need to rescue her." After Charlotte left, purposely not telling me where she went or why, clearly not wanting my help. My back teeth groaned as I clenched my jaw against my next words. "I was about to come see you. To submit a request to search for her."

Liar, liar.

Applegate's lips scrunched into a cruel smile. "Request denied."

Grumble, mumble. "Her life is in danger."

The smile widened. "Request denied."

B.I.T.C.H.

"I'll be dealing with sorcerers," I said, shaking a little from the effort it took to resist screaming at her. But I would not back down. Would. Not. "Since you have no jurisdiction over sorcery, you can't stop me."

"If you're in my territory," she snarled, "request denied."

Oh. My. Freaking—

"Council Leader." Sunny's power rippled as her own temper rose. "You are being unreasonable."

How much of Margaret Applegate remained and how much was Brotherhood? I wished at that moment I could help her, really, truly did. For, as Sunny spoke, I saw the first sign of what I recognized in Mom not so long ago: the way her power fought her, how she struggled for control, her round body dipping slightly as her magic writhed, so much the toes of her practical shoes almost touched the ground. Proof enough for me, if not for others.

Confirmation, absolute confirmation, she was under the Brotherhood's control. And was fighting them just like Mom did.

Only she didn't have me to free her, to give her back

her own magic, a talisman like the pentagram necklace Mom gifted me when I was a teenager. The very one which broke her from the hold of the dark sorcerers. I watched with a sinking heart as Margaret Applegate battled for control.

And lost.

Inevitable, really. If my mother, the most powerful witch I knew, outside myself, couldn't defeat the Brotherhood's hold, there was no way Margaret Applegate could manage it. At least, not alone.

I really need to try. Not just for Charlotte's sake, but for all of ours. Mom was planning a giant conclave of all the world territories this coming summer, but it might be too late by then. I understood her reasoning. She wanted everyone in one place, to check all of the Council Leaders for Brotherhood influence, but waiting another six months could mean the difference between winning and losing this war with the sorcerers.

Beg. My vampire's tone came out sharp-edged.

Sorry? I felt my eyes widen at the very thought, still staring at Applegate as she settled back into her scowl of hate.

Crawl, plead, give her the satisfaction of knowing she's beaten you. My vampire sighed. *As painful an exercise as it might be, Charlotte is worth it.*

Gulp. Oh *hell* no. And yet, I had a terrible feeling she was right.

Remember, she sent as my demon thrashed and cursed, Shaylee huffing in fury while the family magic pooled sadly, *this is Liander Belaisle you're dealing with. His arrogance might lead her to slip.*

Or, it could just lead to me making a total fool of myself.

I'd rather eat my shoes, I snarled. *But I'll try it.*

My vampire actually felt surprised. *Thank you for trusting me*, she sent.

Yeah, well, if you're wrong, I'll never forgive you.

Fair enough, she sent. *I won't forgive myself.*

I reached for Sunny to give her the heads up, adding Shenka to the conversation.

Just back me up, I sent to them before falling to one knee in front of Applegate and allowing my worry for Charlotte to appear. At first, I had to force myself to show vulnerability, but the shock on Applegate's face was enough encouragement as I clasped my hands together under my chin.

"Please," I said, choking now on my rising tears. "Please, I beg you. I'll follow whatever rules you ask, do whatever you want. But allow me to find Charlotte." Hot, fat tears dripped from my chin as I let out the pain I'd been feeling since the weregirl left me.

I'm not sure what I was expecting, but the effect on Applegate was a little bit of a miracle. She sighed, her evil smile fading, a smirk of satisfaction taking its place. But when she spoke, I saw the woman I'd first met shining in her eyes, as though the Brotherhood's power had been somehow appeased by my willingness to show weakness.

A truth I filed away for later. Surely, there was a way to use it to my advantage.

"Well now," she said, coming to hover over me, staring down her round button nose through the glasses perched on its end. "I see you've finally learned to respect your betters. Humility becomes you."

Oh, she's pushing it. I held onto my vampire for support.

She is, she whispered, *but you're winning.*

Passive resistance. Got it.

Applegate tapped her chin with one pudgy finger, rolling her eyes skyward, humming softly as though considering my request. I actually held my breath as she did.

This better work.

My vampire, tense and coiled inside me, didn't answer.

When Applegate finally met my eyes, I thought I lost.

"Very well," she said, crooked teeth gleaming as my heart leaped and did a dance in my chest. "Under certain… conditions."

Ruh-ro.

She lowered herself further, bending in half, her face in mine, the scent of garlic and something fishy wafting over me. Mixed with excessive amounts of baby powder.

Gross.

"You are not, under any circumstances, permitted to use witch magic while in my territory." Her cheeks pinked as she tapped my nose with the same finger she'd used on her own face. "Which means no maji power, either, as your full strength is tied to all of your magicks, correct?" Another tap.

If she touched me again, I was going to break that finger off and feed it to her.

"At the merest sniff of trouble," she snuffled the air, made a face as though my scent offended her rather than the other way around, "I am kicking your ass out of Europe." She looked up at Sunny. "Permanently." Malice laced the sweet smile she fixed on me. "Do you think you can manage to stay out of trouble, Miss Hayle?"

Nice of her to drop my title.

Temper, Sydlynn, my vampire sent. *We're almost free.*

"I think so," I said out loud while tossing a few choice swears internally.

Applegate retreated with a snort. "I highly doubt it," she said. "Thank you for providing me with the means necessary to finally rid myself of your presence."

Ah, my vampire sent. *Well, better this than nothing.*

Nice someone thought so.

Besides, my demon growled, *we're just going to veil in, grab Charlotte and veil out. End of story, nothing to see here, move along.*

I stood as Applegate backed off.

With my track record? Yeah. Sure. Charlotte's rescue would go that smoothly.

I was so screwed.

chapter eight

"Before you tell me to go home," Shenka said as I turned away to the pressure of air displacement at Applegate's departure, "you can just take that and shove it."

I knew this was going to be a fight. "I need you with the family," I said, aiming for reasonable and diplomatic. No use trying for bossy. Not with Shenka.

"You need me beside you," she snapped while Sunny joined us, Uncle Frank's smirk wiped clean as I glared at him.

"Listen to me." I gripped her upper arms, stared into Shenka's determined eyes. "Where do you think you'll do the most good: with the family, watching over them, or with me, unable to use magic?"

Shenka's mouth opened. Closed. Her frown turned sad, still mixed with stubborn. "That's not fair."

"Nope," I said. "It sure as hell isn't. But the sad fact is I have access to other magicks and you don't."

She deflated. "And if I came with you, I'd be a liability." Shenka perked briefly. "But Applegate didn't order me not to use magic."

Sophistry and we both knew it. "You want to start a war over a technicality?" Low blow, Syd, using my vampire's tactics against my own second.

You're learning, my vampire sent.

Shenka hummed and Shenka fumed, but in the end, she left with one of Sunny's vampires giving her an unhappy ride home. With one less person to worry about, I turned back to the vampire queen to find Isabelle waiting beside her.

"I'll take you to your friend," the young vampire said. "But I can't promise retrieving her will be easy."

What in my life was ever easy?

"Just give me a second." I spun away, took a few steps to distance myself, reached for Mom. This conversation could go one of two ways and I was hoping she hadn't had a major backslide since I saw her Friday morning.

Syd, sweetheart, what's wrong? That was my mother. Could sniff trouble from three thousand miles away. Or maybe she just expected it now.

Lovely. Her daughter, the harbinger of impending doom.

Mom, I sent, keeping my emotions as tightly wrapped as possible, *it's Charlotte.*

Like I said, it could go two ways. As I filled her in on the last few minutes of my life, I ran over the possibilities in my mind. One, she would go ballistic on me and demand I come home. But that was the old Mom, right? Two, she would sympathize and tell me to be careful.

Sydlynn Thaddea Hayle, Mom sent, making me wince. She only used my full name when she was pissed. So it was number one. Craptastic.

Wasn't expecting a third option.

You go get that girl and bring her back here so I can have a firm talk with her. She paused. *And kick some ass while you're at it.*

Um. What?

Who are you and what have you done with my mother? I choked on a laugh.

Charlotte is family, Mom sent, a soft waver in her firm tone. *We don't let anything happen to family.*

Agreed. And the ass kicking?

Sorcerers, Mom growled. *They have it coming.*

Holy blessed halleluiah angels with trumpets and sparkly wings.

Mom, I sent. *I love you like whoa.*

Syd, she sent back, the image of her behind her desk, smiling, arms hugging herself, flashed in my mind even as her power embraced me. *Be safe.*

And she was gone.

I turned to find Sunny and Uncle Frank watching me with confused expressions.

"I have orders to go kick some sorcerer ass," I said. "And I can't disobey my Council Leader, can I?"

Uncle Frank laughed. "You've come a long way from making Mir cry, Syd."

Well, we'd see. There was still room for mayhem and world-crumbling disaster.

"Okay then," I said, rubbing my hands together, partly for warmth, feeling a grin stretch my lips. Yes, the outlook was possibly dire, but Mom was behind me and I was feeling rather optimistic, thanks. After all, I didn't need witch or maji power to ride the veil. Just like my demon said, in and out. I offered my hand to Isabelle. "Shall we go liberate one weregirl from the bad guys?"

Oh, how I wish she'd just taken my damned hand and not hesitated. Just one more second, and we'd have been gone. But Isabelle's momentary pause was lengthened by the sudden displacement of air, the calling card of Enforcer power. I spun, snarling, expecting Applegate, a renege on her promise. Only to find a young female witch and an Enforcer settling to the floor.

The pretty blonde with pale hazel eyes bobbed a quick curtsy. "Coven Leader Hayle," she said in a tight British accent, "it's an honor to meet you."

"And you are?" Way to be nice to the new kids, Syd.

Yeah, wasn't really in the mood for nice.

The young witch didn't flinch, earning kudos from me. "My name is Gwendolyn Ravensdale," she said, smiling a little, dimples showing. She turned, gestured to the tall Enforcer beside her. "This is my partner, Finlay Wright."

Okay, he wasn't just tall. He was massive. I knew some big men, like my Dad. But this young Enforcer looked like he could take on a steam engine and win.

"Coven Leader," he said, voice the thunder roll I more associated with my black hound friend Galleytrot than any mortal witch.

"Nice to meet you." I crossed my arms over my chest, scowling back and forth between them. "Now, what do you want?"

So friendly. Yeah, yeah. Stop judging. I had work to do.

Gwendolyn finally showed nerves, just a flash, but enough I felt a little guilty. After all, neither of them felt like sorcery to me, and until I knew what they were doing here, I really didn't have reason to treat them badly.

Until she opened her mouth again.

"We're here to escort you." She glanced sideways at her companion. "Our Council Leader ordered it."

Oh *hell* no.

"You can tell your Council Leader," I said. Stopped. Drew a breath. "Just. Freaking. Lovely."

So much for stealth.

"We are to accord you every courtesy." She seemed to think I gave a crap about courtesy.

Do you want me to detain them? Sunny's mental voice snapped in my head.

The idea was so tempting I almost said yes. "Did your Council Leader say anything else?"

Gwendolyn nodded, face set. "We are to watch you and ensure you fulfill your side of the agreement." She shifted from one foot to the other. "I'm afraid our presence is mandatory."

I guess that answers your question, I sent to Sunny even as I faced the pair of European witches head on and opened my sorcery. The black petals bloomed open, hungry, searching for sustenance, but I held the power back, instead only allowed it to sniff over the two.

It could have been seen as an attack. But while I wouldn't risk checking out Applegate, I had no intention of allowing this pair to tag along if they were also under Brotherhood influence. Since I wasn't breaking Applegate's stupid rules, they could just suck it up.

Neither of them seemed to notice I did anything at all. As I closed off my sorcery, I bit my lower lip, thinking fast. They were clean of the Brotherhood's influence unless it was buried so deep I couldn't find it. But why would Applegate send these two, knowing they weren't under control?

Could she have done so to show me she still fought the Brotherhood's power? Tried to help me somehow?

There was no way of knowing. But at least these two wouldn't sabotage me, not on purpose, anyway.

"Fine," I said, temper barely held in check. "But if either of you does anything to jeopardize the rescue of my werefriend, I won't be responsible for my actions."

Gwendolyn winced slightly. "Ah," she said, "as to the term 'rescue'…"

Now what?

"We've also been instructed to ensure you use proper diplomatic channels in approaching the Czar and his people." She had the good manners to allow regret to cross her expression. "I'm sorry."

Isabelle made an anxious face and shook her head at me. Got the message, loud and clear. The Czar wasn't into diplomacy.

"And if talks fail?" This was turning into an absolute disaster.

"Then they fail." Finlay's deep voice was ice chips and gravel. "And you go home."

chapter nine

So much for sneaking in, grabbing Charlotte from the clutches of her captors, and sneaking out again. Instead, I was forced to allow Finlay to handle transportation, his Enforcer magic cradling both Isabelle and myself along with his partner.

"You don't have to come." I wanted to give the vampire girl an out since she looked almost sick at the prospect of joining me. But she shook her head immediately.

"I won't let you go alone," she said. "I know how they think and might be useful." Her hesitation told me there was a lot more she wasn't saying and I refused to go into this without all the information I needed.

I pulled her aside, glaring at the pair of witches to back off a second, which they did. I heard Sunny engage them in conversation, though what she talked about was lost to me as I focused on Isabelle.

"So this is going to be bad, then?" There was no other explanation for her reaction.

"I'm afraid so," she said. "The Czar might allow you to enter. But he considers himself autonomous—worse, he thinks he is Creator. A god, above all others." She shuddered delicately. "I maintained contact with some of my family, through the years. The Black Souls are extremely long lived, and Yure Danko has been their leader since the fall of their beloved Rasputin a century ago. Unfortunately, their own careful breeding program since the beginning of their order has meant each leader has grown progressively more insane as their blood lines mingle too closely. Yure is the worst of them all, but he is, sadly, also brilliant."

"Which means by walking in the front door, we're just putting Charlotte at risk." I sighed. Just what I needed. A moldy old sorcerer with a god complex. "Are we sure she is at risk? That she's actually a captive? She left me voluntarily."

Wasn't bitter or anything. But it still hurt.

Still.

Isabelle sighed. "I don't know for certain," she said. "She came to Yure of her own free will, but from what I've been told, she was coerced. Is she there now by choice?" She let out a quick breath despite the fact she didn't need to breathe, a fall back to her time as a mortal.

"I don't think so. And knowing the Black Souls as I do, knowing Yure, he's holding something over her." She looked like she was going to go on, but shook her head instead and fell quiet.

I really didn't think Charlotte was there by choice either. Charlotte spent her life with the Dumonts, had been their slave for years. I couldn't see her trading one nasty family for another, not for any reason. And yet, how well did I know her, really?

Only one way to find out.

"Here's the deal," I said, lowering my voice even further. "If this fails, I'm going in to get her. But I'll need you to distract the Tweedles." Dee and Dumb, though I doubted the labels applied, had to be prepared for such an event. Applegate would have made sure of that.

Isabelle didn't look happy. "I can't be seen," she said. "Or recognized. There could be repercussions." Whatever that meant.

I can glamour her, Shaylee sent. *If you think my Sidhe power can block their sorcery.*

I shared the offer with Isabelle who looked suddenly less anxious.

"They will not think to look for me," she said, "and will have no reason to focus on me if your Sidhe magic keeps them distracted." She nodded sharply. "Very well, we will try it." Her lips lifted in a little smile. "Just give me some warning before you start a war."

75

"Same for you," I said.

Isabelle arched both eyebrows, all innocence.

Fair enough.

I left her, rejoined my escorts. "I'm ready," I said. "Let's ride."

I swear I had never been so cold. Not ever. Bitterly, chillingly, so flipping freezing my skin burned. The second Finlay landed us in the squeaky snow, I started shivering uncontrollably and not even a burst of demon heat warmed me.

I was so busy dying of hypothermia I almost missed the two giant, armed men standing at a towering, black iron gate. Considering they were right in front of us, not spotting them right away was quite a feat. But between my demon wailing over the cold, the fact my feet were already numb and the rest of me felt like I'd been dipped in an ice bath, I had a hard time focusing on anything but the chattering of my teeth.

Good thing Shaylee was more focused than I was. When I glanced sideways at Isabelle, I almost choked. Because the young vampire wasn't there anymore. Only a vaguely attractive young woman my eyes drifted sideways from as though she wasn't interesting.

Sorry, Shaylee sent, easing up, allowing me to see through the glamour. *I got excited.*

No—chatter—*problemo*—chatter.

"Coven Leader Sydlynn Hayle," Gwendolyn said as she stepped forward, not a shiver in sight. "Here to speak to your leader."

The guards exchanged a dull, empty stare before ignoring her. Were they wearing fur? Real fur? While the idea disgusted me, I immediately coveted their plush hats and massive jackets. Not so much their large, black guns.

But these were werewolves. When my demon finally generated enough heat I could function, I recognized the fact, the wolves in them familiar thanks to my time spent with Charlotte.

What did weres need with machine guns?

It wasn't until Finlay put himself between them, blue Enforcer magic crackling, the pair actually paid attention. And the threat he presented only generated a minor act. Guard number one pulled a two-way from his pocket and spoke into it. In Ukrainian, I guessed. Sounded like the language Charlotte let slip now and again. Static crackled before a voice came through. Isabelle tensed beside me as the guard let his hand drop.

"*Hi,*" he said. The word sounded like "knee". What was wrong with his knee?

"'*Hi*' means no," Isabelle whispered.

Splutter.

Like hell.

My surging anger did more to warm me up than any magic as I shoved my way into the armed guard's face.

Yes, it meant rising on my tiptoes while he stared down at me with his flat, cold expression. Sure, I probably looked ridiculous, half his size and red-faced from the cold.

Didn't care. Amber fire crackled around me, sizzling the snow beneath my feet into clouds of steam, the mist rising to flare in the sheets of flame my demon provided. Wolf eyes flickered across dark brown as I finally got the big jerk's attention.

"Move your ass," I said, "or I'll move it for you."

Please. Don't move.

Guard number two entered my peripheral vision, probably coming to his friend's rescue. A surge of Sidhe earth magic rocked the ground under his feet, exploding upward, sending him flying back, his gun landing with a soft thud in the snow even as the ground beneath him steamed before giving way, a quicksand pit swallowing him to his hips.

"Coven Leader!" I didn't have to look to know Gwendolyn's face had to be pinched in shock, because from the choked sound of her voice coming from behind me, things weren't going as she'd planned.

Yeah, diplomacy and I didn't get along very well. And I hated being told no.

The first guard must have decided he needed to take me seriously at last, because I felt his body tense, shift, just before I opened to my vampire and let her out. Snarling, spirit power flaring in a corona so bright he cried out. She shoved him hard, back against the iron gate, pinning him. He fought us, battled for control while his friend shouted something in Ukrainian into his own two-way, still trying to pull himself free of the sucking ground Shaylee created.

Let them send reinforcements. I was already irritated by this whole mess. I'd take them all on.

Coven Leader. Finlay's mental connection flared bright blue as he forced his way into my mind. *An incident will mean your expulsion from Europe permanently.*

Damn it.

Just. Damn. It.

I backed off, reeling in my demon, my vampire sighing her frustration as Shaylee pouted, solidifying the ground around the other guard as she retreated. Too late, I heard the roar of an engine, knew I'd stepped over the line and just doomed Charlotte and myself to alternatives I wasn't sure I was prepared to follow through.

Screw that. Applegate could start her ridiculous war. I was getting my friend out of there if it was the last thing I did.

The large military vehicle roared to a halt on the other side of the gate, the passenger door slamming while a dozen or so werewolves in fatigues and carrying guns leaped from the back of the covered truck and formed a line with their weapons trained on me.

Like shooting at me would do them any good.

Though I supposed guns would impress others. But at this point, I'd broken Applegate's rule. Which meant, I could now use maji power.

Poor little wereboys and girls. They had no idea they didn't stand a chance.

A tall figure pushed his way through the line, coming to stand a foot or so from the gate. Flat, gray eyes looked me up and down, glanced sideways at the guard writhing, up to his waist in freezing earth. At the one who denied my entry. Back to me.

His angular features and long, thin nose made him look more fox-like than wolf, and though he was bundled in as much fur as the others, I could tell he was leaner, too. But to me, no less dangerous.

More so, if I knew his type. And when I reached for him, I realized my mistake. Not a werewolf at all. The black emptiness of him told me what I needed to know.

Sorcerer.

"*Вітаємо*," he said, before switching to heavily accented English. "Be welcome, Coven Leader Hayle."

Um, okay.

"I'm totally getting 'hey, how are you' from your little show here," I said. Gwendolyn hissed behind me, a warning most likely. Whatever.

A thin smile cracked the sorcerer's lips, pulling at the deep dimple in his chin. "We are not used to accepting visitors. Especially ones so esteemed."

His words might have been complimentary, but I still got the dirt bag vibe from him.

"I'm here to talk to Yure Danko," I said. "I was told 'no'." I leaned closer to the gate, letting my demon rumble her unhappiness in my eyes. "I don't do 'no'."

Another smile, wider, though those gray eyes were as cold as ever. "An unfortunate error," he said. Bowed slightly. "I am Vasyl Krajnik, the Czar's head of security. I am more than happy to escort you," again his eyes traveled, this time over my shoulder at my companions before snapping back to me, "to meet his Royal Majesty."

So maybe my rule-breaking moment wasn't one after all. No incident, no retaliation from Applegate. And though I was sure I was in for a show and a whole heap of disappointment, the leader of the European Council had bound my hands.

Show it was. Pass the popcorn.

CHAPTER TEN

I would have preferred to walk, on principle, but, frankly, felt happy for the ride in the warm back of the big, black SUV arriving only a moment after the gates swung open. I ignored the show of power Vasyl brought with him, the line of wereguards turning with trained precision to follow my every move. At least the muzzles of their guns were lowered. Well, half lowered.

Either this was their usual or I scared the bejeebuz out of them.

I chose to think the latter.

The heavy door thudded shut behind me, warmth enveloping me as the blast of heat from the leather seat radiated upward into my freezing behind. I almost snarled at the loss of precious heat as the door behind me opened, Gwendolyn slipping inside with Finlay next to her. Isabelle didn't give Vasyl a chance to sit next to me in the second row, firmly closing her door on his face. I caught enough of his scowl through the black tinted glass I worried he'd seen through her glamour though Shaylee calmly informed me all was well and I had to trust her.

From the glare Isabelle leveled at him, however, I knew the pair had history. Just as long as that history didn't interfere with my rescue of Charlotte, Isabelle could keep her secrets.

Vasyl slammed the front passenger door and snapped something at the driver. The SUV's engine purred as we turned and drove off, the amazing suspension rumbling smoothly over the snow-covered lane.

"His Royal Majesty is most eager to meet you," Vasyl said over his shoulder. "Though perhaps some indication of your purpose for this visit would make your introduction go more smoothly?"

No way he didn't know why I was there. Come on, sharkboy. Did they really think I was that stupid? Besides, I highly doubted the Czar was happy I'd crashed his little ego party. "I'm just here to see your boss," I said. "No time for small talk."

"With those beneath me," went unsaid. Because, I was classy like that.

Vasyl turned to smile at me despite my silent rebuke, a shark smile of bright white teeth and cold gray eyes. "As you wish." He turned back again, voice full of dark humor. "I'm sure your visit will be most enlightening."

Like I didn't know I was walking into some kind of trap. So he really did think I was a total idiot.

Sheesh. Bad guys had serious underestimation issues.

I stared out the window, evergreen trees heavy with thick, white blankets flashing by as we wound through the Ukrainian countryside. I expected a short drive up a lane to some kind of mansion. Instead, we were on the road a solid five minutes, silence heavy and hanging in the cab of the SUV. I felt the tickle of Gwendolyn's mind as she politely tried to get me to talk to her, but I shut her out.

No time to be a wilting princess. I was pretty sure she'd only tell me to back off and be less aggressive. She didn't know me at all.

Was about to have another lesson in Sydology as the SUV turned a corner and roared down the last stretch of road.

I caught glimpses of stone and something truly massive, but it wasn't until the truck came to a halt, the door beside me opening in a whoosh, icy air washing over me, I realized this was no mansion. Or castle, either, Wilhelm's seat having nothing on this place.

My feet slipped on the snow as I stepped out, gaping at the massive palace stretched out before me, the climbing columns reminding me of the entry to Widener Library at Harvard. But bigger. And capped with more columns, rising another four or five stories. All from cream stone that looked like marble.

Okay then. I had to admit I was impressed. But not by the Czar—by the people who built this place.

Holy. I bet astronauts saw it from space.

I followed Vasyl, my companions and about an army's worth of werewolves trailing behind me through the thin layer of snow over the cobbled drive and up the steps. No winter leavings here, meticulously swept clean from the deep purple carpeting lining the stairway. Talk about extravagant. I was used to the vampires and their elegant attempt at recreating the past. But this place made me think of old world Russia I learned about in history class, like time rewound—or at least stood still—in this place. An era where opulence and decadence reined as much as the Czars.

At least the interior felt warm, though I'd hate to have the heat bill. Towering double doors groaned shut behind us, the deep burgundy wood polished and shining. Elaborate handles larger than my hands could grasp twisted with silver and gold vines. My feet squeaked once as they touched stone, only to fall silent again on the runner of matching purple carpet beginning at the threshold and running deep into the massive cave of the entry.

No, not cave. More like a cathedral, all sconces and statues and filigree gold, like I was standing on the inside of a Faberge egg. Cream marble, giant portraits, a chandelier dripping so much crystal I could barely look at it. Sure, I'd read about places like this, seen a few in movies and the like, but actually standing there, surrounded by so much wealth so blatantly displayed drove a spike of anger through my stomach.

How many people were hurt, made to suffer, or left by the wayside to create this place? What I knew of Russian history did nothing to cool my rising temper.

Vasyl paused, giving me time to be all awed and stuff. Seriously.

"Nice place," I said. "Oh, by the way." I strode past him, "your self-esteem issues are showing."

Snap.

I could tell the wereguards weren't all that happy about me taking the lead, but I'd had it. Up. To. Here. With all of this crap. I aimed myself at another set of double doors that seemed to be under heavy protection and headed in that direction, the full length of the giant foyer between me and them, my temper only rising with each step.

Please. Gwendolyn finally made it through. *I know, I really do. But think of your friend.*

I am, I snapped back. *Now, either keep your opinions to yourself, or leave. Pick one.*

I shut her down even as I strode closer to the target doors.

The guards didn't move, faced me down. More gathered. I had the right place, at least. But the closer I approached, the more determined I was to get through and I was not stopping.

Not.

So they'd better get their furry asses out of my way or I'd be playing ten-pin bowling with their big, ugly heads.

No demon this time, no vampire. And not Shaylee, either, though I held her in reserve. This place was pretty and everything, but a nicely place earthquake would do wonders for the décor.

Instead, I opened up the black flower beneath me, accessing my sorcery, allowing it to bloom, its hunger alive, reaching.

Ready to feed.

While using my sorcery still gave me the creeps, this seemed an appropriate time to whip it out, considering who I was about to confront. Best Yure Danko understood I wasn't screwing around.

Ten steps. The guards stiffened. Nine steps. They raised their weapons. Eight. They tightened ranks. Seven. Blackness, pooled at my feet, began to expand outward, reaching for the hot, bubbling power of the werewolves, starving for their essence. Six. Five.

Four.

Three.

Close enough to see fear in their eyes, the slight tremor of their weapons. So they were afraid.

Wicked.

Two.

"*Стояти осторонь.*" Vasyl's voice echoed in the air, just over my right shoulder. "Let her through."

One.

The line of guards parted like a wave before the prow of a ship. My sorcery licked at the edges of the slower ones, tasting them. I watched them pale, felt a little sick, but refused to show it. Instead, I stopped and lifted my arm, gestured, drawing on my power to open the doors.

Shaylee responded.

My demon.

My vampire.

My sorcery.

Oops.

Good thing I was shielding. The resulting explosion was quiet impressive, if I do say so myself. I had enough time to realize the girls were just a little too pissed off for this to end well, and extended my shielding outward to gather the pieces of shattered doorway, capturing them in a bubble of spirit magic before my demon set them on fire. They flared in bursts of spark even as Shaylee, not to be outdone, wiggled her way past them and sent a rumble through the floor of the palace just strong enough to make the chandelier behind me tinkle in response.

Way to make an entrance, Hayle. And though I hadn't intended for this to happen, the girls took my gesture and their own irritation and turned it into something absolutely spectacular.

I let the bubble of wards collapse as the ash from the remains of the door, now a sifting pile of dust, cascaded to the floor on the other side. Shivering a little from just how freaking awesome and scary that was, doing my best to hide my own shock at the total overreaction of my alter egos, I stuck my hands in my pockets and strolled through the gap like I'd been invited inside.

CHAPTER ELEVEN

More elaborate decorating greeted me, the giant throne room's ceiling arching overhead with painted murals of battle scenes and old kings and queens. The cream marble floor gleamed on either side of the continuing carpet. Talk about an arrow shot to the seat of power. Any dummy could find Yure Danko.

Just follow the purple shag road.

I didn't hurry. Needed time to assess the situation anyway. Not only that, I wanted the so-called Czar to sweat out my approach. He watched me, or I assumed it was he, from a massive gold throne at the other end of the room. A line of werewolves stood on either side of the carpet, their sullen wolf energy making my skin crawl. Worse was the emptiness as a handful of sorcerers from the Czar's sect joined them. I kept my eyes fixed on Yure while my alter egos explored the room for me, filtering information while I maintained my steady, casual pace.

There are too many to fight, Shaylee sent. *But a quake would even the odds.*

Agreed. My vampire sighed. *I believe your temper is rubbing off on me, Sydlynn. That was a horribly impulsive thing to do.*

Oh, you think? It was hard to keep my lips from twisting into a grin.

Whiners, my demon snarled. *Just let me at them.*

Easy, tiger, I sent. *Let's see where our show of power gets us before we run off half-cocked.*

Again, my vampire sent. *Run off half-cocked* again.

Smartass hitchhiker.

I felt someone join me, caught sight of Vasyl striding forward to match my pace, the pair of us coming to a halt at the bottom of the three steps leading to the throne as a matched set. Well, as matched as I could get with him towering over me.

"Your Royal Majesty," Vasyl swept into a bow, "may I present Coven Leader Sydlynn Hayle, all the way from America."

Part of me wanted to be impressed by the Czar. After all, dude ran most of Europe with his organized mob system and his bullyboy selection of werewolves hand-raised to do his bidding. But the small, balding man perched on the edge of the massive throne reminded me more of an irritated squirrel than a great leader. At some point, someone should have suggested he try braces for those buck teeth he had going on, and maybe a good scrubbing would clean the shine from his greasy, pockmarked face. Though, for someone over a hundred years old, if Isabelle was to be believed, he didn't look a day over fifty.

I'm sure the smile he aimed in my direction was meant to make me feel in awe of his greatness. Instead, it just made me queasy.

Pretty apparent he'd had something black and green for lunch.

"We expected your arrival," Yure said as he hunched forward, the heavy purple robe he wore pulling across his chest. Gold clanked, the gaudy medallion on a chain as thick as my wrist clattering when he moved. "For quite some time now. You may bow before us."

Did he seriously just talk about himself in "Royal we"?

"I've been busy," I said. He could take my lack of genuflecting and shove it. "With more important things."

Sizzle, my demon sent.

Think of Charlotte, my vampire hissed.

Go for the throat, Shaylee sent.

Helpful bunch.

The Black Souls leader sat back, smile turned surly, bulging, muddy eyes showing even more white. "So you say." He gripped the carved arms of his throne with his girly hands, nails chewed to the quick. His pasty face went mottled a moment, patches of red flickering over his cheeks and down his throat. I felt the bubbling blackness of his sorcery emerge, press against mine. "And yet, despite your so-called power, you have as yet to defeat your enemy."

I wasn't here to trade insults with a crazy dude. "Whatever," I said. Took a leap of intuition and prodded him to see how much he'd already uncovered. "You know why I'm here."

This was the mafia we were talking about. He probably had damned Russian hackers diving into my private life as I stood there, all up in my business.

Another smile, this one tight and cruel. He steepled his hands before him, resting his elbows on his round stomach and struck a classic bad-guy pose. It took all the strength I had not to sigh and roll my eyes.

I was so over this already.

"Perhaps we do," he said. "But we would like to hear you beg."

I'd already been forced to plead for Charlotte once today. No way was I doing it again. Especially not in front of this charlatan and his little god show.

"I'm here for my wereguard," I said, slamming against his power with mine while the girls tensed inside me. "Give her back and I'll leave peacefully."

Gwendolyn's anxiety was palpable, coming at me in waves from over my right shoulder. The girl really had to learn to hold in her crap or at least shield properly. Then again, she hadn't exactly been prepared for this, I didn't think.

I had to thank Margaret Applegate for sending rank amateurs along for the ride.

Even as Yure reacted, I understood the European Council Leader's strategy. She could have sent more seasoned witches as backup/guides/babysitters, but she wanted me to fail. To have an excuse to kick me out of her territory forever. To start a war, likely, one the Brotherhood could use to their advantage.

"Your wereguard." He was still smiling, even more deeply. Yeah, his lunch leftovers were turning my stomach. "You claim her?"

"I do," I said. "We're bonded." Okay, so not exactly true anymore. Actually, not true at all from what I could tell. But we had been. That had to count for something.

"Is that so?" The sorcerer wriggled in his chair like a chubby puppy eager to play. "Well then, in that case, we have made a terrible error." He clapped his hands, gestured at Vasyl. "Bring her." His eyes fixed on me again, power pushing, pushing. "Her *пов'язана одна* awaits."

Me, presumably. This could be bad. My vampire stilled. *I'm certain Charlotte isn't bonded to us any longer.*

So? My demon's anger sizzled. *We remake the bond and get the hell out of here.*

If it is that easy, Shaylee sent, *why didn't Charlotte do so previously?*

Maybe she didn't want to be bonded to us anymore. That truth hurt. A lot. But I had to offer it up.

I fear there is more to this than we know, my vampire sent, her worry rising to the surface of my mind.

Her worry was mutual.

Yure must have been keeping Charlotte close, because it was only a moment later a large door opened on my right. I turned toward it, knowing my eagerness was a sign of weakness, but unable to help myself. I caught a glimpse of Gwendolyn's unhappy face before I locked my gaze on Charlotte.

chapter twelve

She looked fine, at least physically, as she approached with her head down, held firmly between two of her fellow weres, the males towering over her. Her long, blonde hair had been cut to her shoulders, her normal leather jacket and skinny jeans replaced by a rather frumpy dress. Just seeing Charlotte in a skirt made me wince. Even when she'd accompanied me to the court of the vampire queens, she'd refused to wear one. Whatever Yure had done to her had to be nasty if she willingly wore all that ugly pink satin and ruffled lace.

Charlotte didn't look up, hands clasped before her, bound with heavy cuffs. A choker of the same metal hugged her neck. She looked so weak, frail, compared to the powerful, stoic girl I knew, I wanted to reach for her, but I held off, looking up to glare at Yure as she was pulled up the first step to stand with her back to him.

He giggled in evil glee, reaching out to prod Charlotte between the shoulder blades with the toe of his boot. Well, tried to. I hit him so hard the moment I realized what he was doing, he pressed back into his throne with a grunt.

"Don't." I hit him again. "Touch." And one more time, even as the weres around me growled as they finally realized I was the source of their leaders discomfort. "Her."

I let him go even as Vasyl waved the protective guards back. His shark eyes blinked once, slowly, as though in approval of my act.

Now that was interesting.

Yure's red face bloomed like a rotten flower, spit flying from his lips as he jabbed a finger—and his sorcery—at me. "YOU DARE!"

My shields met his hit and repelled it easily, even as I let the bubble of wards slide backward to protect the witches and vampire who accompanied me, and forward to hug Charlotte.

"I do," I said. Snarled, my demon forcing her fury out of me. "You touch her again and I'll rip your heart out and eat it whole."

Syd. Syd. What the hell? Yeah, my temper was going to get us killed.

What else was new?

Yure lurched to his feet, spluttering, losing his crap.

And I'm certain, if it hadn't been for Vasyl, I would have been fighting an army of werewolves in three, two, one—

"Your Most Royal Majesty." Vasyl's power joined ours, slipping along the side of his leader's. "The test?"

Yure spun on his security head, fury still at full throttle. But it eased visibly as the other sorcerer calmly siphoned off his leader's rage. I watched through the touch of our power, fascinated, noting the shark-like Vasyl absorbed the other man's anger to feed his own dark blossom.

I added that little tidbit to my lineup of questions for Demetrius. I knew sorcery worked by destroying objects, even people, by drawing out the natural power they held. But I had no idea extreme emotion could also be a source of fuel.

Which made me wonder who was the real power here. And think of the Brotherhood.

Focus, Syd.

Yure finally sank back into his throne, the wereguards standing down, though they remained tense and snarling. Let them. I met Vasyl's eyes and cocked an eyebrow before turning back to the glaring Czar.

"Let her go," I said.

"Our faithful Vasyl is correct." Yure spat every word, the acid of his tone burning the air. "The test."

What test? "Fine," I said. "Whatever." I saw Charlotte twitch, the first time she'd reacted since she'd been brought out.

Was that excitement or fear? Or something else?

"Fool," Yure said, eyes rolling in triumphant madness. "You've already failed." He gestured at Charlotte. "We've had her back in our possession for months now. Were you still bonded, she would be dead. No true bonded can be separate from their *пов'язана однаfor* more than a few days and survive."

Damn it. So it was true. No more bond. Charlotte's body quivered again.

Well, we really did know that already, my vampire sent. *The question is, can the bond be rebuilt?*

And does Charlotte want it rebuilt. I hated doubting her loyalty. I knew she loved me, she'd come back from the dead for me, left me that note. But she'd left, hadn't she? Without telling me where she was going or why.

Maybe she really didn't want me to save her.

"Charlotte." Screw the weres hovering, threatening. Screw Vasyl and his cold stare. Screw the witches sent to make sure I messed up and the damned false Czar almost foaming at the mouth in pleasure of seeing me fail. I reached for her with my power, but couldn't get to her. A black sheath of slime surrounded her, coating her in filth. I recognized Yure's power, the same touch I still felt, pressed against my own sorcery. "Charlotte," I repeated. "Look at me."

It took her a long time to lift her chin, blonde hair

shielding her face. When she finally did, her blue eyes were dull, lifeless. Devoid of the girl I knew.

What had they done to her? Rage reappeared in a flash of fire, my demon roaring her fury, but I held back, hands trembling with the effort.

"There," Yure said with great satisfaction in his voice. "You see? She is no longer yours. She is ours." His eyes narrowed, cheeks sinking, as he tried for shrewd. "But we will make you an offer." He giggled, wriggled again, clearly getting a sick kick out of the whole thing. "If you can renew the bond, we will allow you to leave peacefully." He snorted, slapped both knees. "With her."

He expected me to fail, that much was glaringly obvious. "And if I can't?"

Yure's humor turned to dark pleasure. He leaned forward, sniffing at Charlotte's hair, though he kept his distance. Was he afraid of me, after all? "You leave," he said. "And the lovely Charlotte becomes my bride."

Um, what? The weregirl's face crumpled. Only a flash of fear and despair, but enough I caught it.

Hell. No.

Any doubt I had she didn't want to be here was gone in a flash of protective anger.

Okay, I sent to the egos inside me. *What do we do now?*

Crickets.

Seriously? My own desperation rose. *We have to save her. None of us really explored the feeling of the bond,* my vampire sent. *We have no idea what it was or how to recreate it.*

It was one-sided, my demon sent. *And subtle. We didn't even know it was there for ages, remember?*

Damn it. No way I was letting Charlotte down.

We have to do something, I sent. *Shaylee?*

I'm sorry, the Sidhe princess sent. I caught a flash of her wringing her hands. *I wish there was something we could do.*

Thanks for nothing. It came out in a snarl, though it wasn't their fault. This was as much mine as anyone's. Why hadn't I pushed Charlotte for answers? Why did I just let her keep her secrets?

She watched me, had to know I struggled with what to do. I had felt the bond, at least briefly. Didn't really understand it at the time, or know how to recreate it. Not without exploring how it felt again. And now that I thought it through, I realized the only magic I'd thought to explore it with was my witch power.

Power I couldn't use.

As my shoulders slumped, Charlotte's chin dipped again, eyes on the floor.

My powers reached for her, tried to force past the sorcery. I even used my own to slice it open, to let the girls inside. But there was nothing to latch onto. I felt the soft thrum of the wolf within Charlotte, but the faint connection we'd had was gone. And I had not a clue as to what to do to remake it. My family magic, forced to remain dormant, was useless. I wasn't even sure I could reform the bond from my end. She'd created it in the first place, hadn't she?

Shaylee dug down deep, her earth power looking for anything to grasp while my vampire spun a sticky spider's web of spirit threads around the weregirl in an effort to pull apart the sorcerous shell and let me at her.

My demon roared in fury, burning the edges of the Czar's containment, singeing herself in the process.

They all faltered, each of them in turn, unable to work together for the first time in a very long time. Without my family magic—that struggled, begged me to allow it to try—our cohesion was broken.

Only my sorcery seemed to connect, oozing around and through Yure's construct, though when it reached Charlotte's mind there was nothing to seize hold of, unless I wanted to fight the Czar for ownership.

I considered it as my demon fell back, panting her fury, Shaylee sending another tremor through the floor as her frustration cracked around the edges. Even my typically level vampire lashed a crackling bolt of spirit power at the base of the throne dais out of sheer irritation.

My sorcery waited, hunger burning, wanting to devour the Czar.

Wanting to devour Charlotte.

Which would mean her trading one master for another. While I could have fought him for her, enslaved her, where would we go from there? And if I did succeed, would she ever forgive me?

Not to mention the fact, if I failed, I doubted Yure Danko would kindly let me retreat from the fight before sucking me dry. And I'd been through that experience before, thanks, under different circumstances but still.

Which meant it was over. We were done.

I finally pulled away, regret burning a hole in the lining of my stomach, heart pounding, glaring up at Yure who laughed out loud.

"As we expected," he said. "So much for your power, witch."

Enough. I was done with this charade. I reached for the family magic hiding behind the girls, ready to call on my maji power and just take her.

Gwendolyn shouldered past me. "We see now our error, Your Royal Majesty," she said while I gaped at her. "Forgive our intrusion. We won't bother you any further."

Yure flicked his fingers at us. "Despite your rude behavior," he said, "we grant you safe passage from our territory." His bulging eyes locked on me. "But if we catch you here again, we will kill every single person you love. And have ever met. Just before we kill you."

Enforcer power engulfed me even as I fought against Finlay as blue magic flared, carrying me away.

chapτer τhirτeen

I fumed as I paced the suite of rooms I'd been assigned, arguing with myself. I could have done more to escape this predicament. How had I gone from rescuing Charlotte—easy peasy in and outsie—to being pinned down by a pair of European stalkers in an ancient hotel in the outback of the Ukraine?

So much grief in so little time. I really should have been used to being imprisoned in fancy quarters. Happened pretty frequently. But this time, I was here by choice.

Okay, not really. I had put my foot down when Finlay tried to deliver me back home, taking a firm hold on his power and forcing him to put us down outside the gates to Yure's territory. For the first time, I saw the young Enforcer's temper flare, but I didn't really give a damn what he thought.

Thanks to him, Charlotte was still back there. And now I knew her fate, no way was I leaving her in Yure's clutches. Not when the girl I knew was so broken she couldn't even fight to protect herself.

"I'm going back in there," I snarled at Finlay and Gwendolyn while Isabelle pushed back the hood of her robe, revealing her pinched features while she stared at the gate as though confused. "And I'm getting Charlotte out."

"No," Finlay said. "You're not."

"Coven Leader," Gwendolyn put herself between me and the hulking brute. Good thing. For him. My demon snapped and snarled her need to launch his ass into orbit while the young witch went on. "Please, don't do this. Our two Councils are on shaky enough ground as it is."

"If you're asking me," I said, jabbing her in the chest with one finger while Finlay growled like a were himself, "to leave Charlotte behind because your Leader happens to have an agenda, you can just forget it."

She flinched. Looked away. How much did she know—suspect? Was she aware Applegate was under sorcerous control? "We will do everything in our power to free your friend," she said, meeting my eyes again. "But I beg you, allow us to handle it."

"I'm not going home." I crossed my arms over my chest, glared at Finlay who glared back. "You're stuck with me until I get Charlotte back. So unless you want that incident you're trying to prevent, I suggest you work fast. I won't wait long."

Gwendolyn seemed relieved, bobbed her head in a nod, nervous smile returning. "As you wish."

Which was how I ended up pacing the top floor of a very old-fashioned hotel. The only hotel, it turned out, in a picturesque town only a few miles from Yure's fenced-in territory. The whole place was a throwback to history. Square, whitewashed buildings lined with balconies, with red tiled roofs lined the streets, octagonal architecture topped with multiple spires towering over the narrow, cobbled ways. I shivered as my anger dissipated, hating how my fear for Charlotte and the choice I had to make caused me to feel colder.

A cheerful older woman and her husband, both dressed in traditional garb, greeted the group of us. Her flowing white blouse and massive black velvet skirt reminded me of Mom, though this woman was almost a head shorter than me and twice as wide. His round belly was tucked behind a wool vest, a cap perched on his balding head. It took me only a heartbeat to realize they were, in fact, witches.

"Yutsk is a coven town," Gwendolyn said as she turned to the couple who bowed to me, faces eager. "*Вітаю*, Nataliya." She gestured to me. "Coven Leader Hayle, this is Coven Leader Nataliya Makosky and her husband, Fedir."

The woman grasped my hand, kissed the back of it, her round cheeks pink, equally round body quivering in what seemed like excitement. *"Вітаємо,* welcome," she said in very thick English. "You come." She pulled me into the building, still clutching my hand, while her husband bowed over and over again.

"They are very honored to have you," Gwendolyn said. "Nataliya may be Coven Leader here in Yutsk, but you are legend."

Seriously? Kind of freaked me out, considering I wasn't even legal to drink back home. I smiled at the woman as I freed my hand. "Thank you," I said, not sure what else to do. Glanced at Gwendolyn. "I'm not supposed to use my magic," I said. "But can I greet her?" Traditionally, Coven Leaders shared a tiny fragment of family magic, a show of respect.

Finlay scowled, but Gwendolyn's face brightened with a relieved smile. "I'm sure such a personal use is fine," she said, kicking her Enforcer's foot.

I turned back to Nataliya and held out my hand again, letting a small ball of blue form over my palm. The family magic came willingly, happily, though I could feel its discomfort at being contained. I soothed it with love and begged for patience while Nataliya's eyes widened. Fingers shaking, she slid hers across my skin, her own small magic mingling with mine.

The family power surged and offered her more than

the usual. She beamed at me, lunged forward, kissing both of my cheeks before turning, arm around me, pulling me tight to her soft body, chattering to her husband in Ukrainian while he smiled at me and bowed yet again.

Thank you, Gwendolyn sent. *That was very generous.*

I didn't do it for you, I sent.

Mean? Totally. So?

I intended to find a small room to use for my base of operations and keep a low profile while I figured out what to do. Didn't go so well. Within moments, the hotel lobby flooded with witches, all come to stare at the visitor. Most didn't speak English and, though I did my best to be polite, playing gracious guest wasn't on my list of things to do at the moment.

Isabelle tucked her cold body next to mine after about twenty minutes of chatter and the beginnings of a tension headache. She spoke to the coven in Ukrainian, translating in my head as she did.

Your welcome is most kind, she sent/said. *The Coven Leader is honored to be among you. But she is weary from her travels and must rest.*

Nataliya clapped her hands abruptly, eyes wide. Reached for me.

Our forgiveness, most revered, Isabelle translated as the witch spoke. *The feast can wait.*

My stomach growled. *Feast?*

Isabelle's eyes met mine. *You're to be made an honorary coven member*, she sent.

How sweet. *Just get me out of here*, I sent. Weariness settled over me, the despair returning.

Within moments, I was moving up the broad staircase, hand running over the blackened wood of the railing, into the darkness of the upstairs. An ancient elevator carried me the rest of the way to the top floor and a giant suite of rooms. The place felt like a Goth girl's dream and made me think of Mia. The arching ceiling heights paired with dark walls. A black canopy loomed over the massive four-poster. Deep gray upholstery of the furniture and heavily patterned area rugs and morbid paintings rounded out the Halloween atmosphere.

I firmly turned my back on Nataliya after three curtsies and a few farewells, letting Isabelle handle the woman while Gwendolyn and Finlay stood together, one of his big hands on her shoulder, watching me.

Isabelle turned after closing the door, leaning against it with a sigh. Again, I found it odd vampires, breathless, used such mundane habits despite themselves.

"They are lovely," she said, a smile lifting her lips. "I'd forgotten the people of my homeland can be so wonderful."

"Charming." Sarcasm came easily as I rubbed my temples with my tense fingers. "I take it pinning my ass to the ground was part of the plan?" They had, effectively.

Yes, I could ride the veil out of here, but any attempt to leave would be noticed, and fast. And I was positive now that an entire coven kept their power locked on me, if only out of curiosity. Their attention would lure Applegate's if I stepped out of line.

Gwendolyn's face fell, whether from guilt or hurt I didn't know. Or care. "We will return shortly," she said. "The coven will protect you." Guard me, she meant. Finlay's little smirk told me as much. "I promised you we would do everything we could to return Charlotte to you. And we will. You just have to trust us."

"Frankly?" I was this close to snapping her in half for being such a freaking idiot. "I don't believe a word you say. Have zero reason."

Gwendolyn's lower lip trembled.

I refused to feel sorry for her. Time to slam them face first into the truth about Applegate and see what shook loose. "Your Council Leader is under the thrall of the Brotherhood." The young witch flinched, but didn't argue. "And you know it." Again, she didn't fight me. Neither did Finlay. "You allow a thralled Leader to dictate your policy and threaten peace between our territories, not to mention the safety of your people." Gwendolyn rocked with every word, as though I struck her physically, while Finlay's lip curled into threatening snarl.

"That's enough," he growled.

"Not by a long shot," I snapped back. "But I'm done

with this conversation considering the fact you're both clearly too weak-minded and brainwashed to actually wake the hell up and do anything about it." I turned my back on them. "You both make me sick." How could they know and not act? How many of the people in this territory knew and did nothing? I clenched my arms tight around my body, shuddering with the need to smack the both of them. "Get out of my sight."

I felt them go. Unwound long enough to kick the back of an antique sofa. The wooden frame cracked, the heavy piece flying across the room to slam into the wall.

Didn't help. Worth a try, though. Maybe breaking a few other things would do the job.

"I have my own investigating to do," Isabelle said. I spun to face her, startled. Forgot she was there. Her frown of curiosity triggered a memory and broke my fury in half.

"What?" It was only three steps to cross to her side. She shook her head as I came to a stop in front of her.

"The Czar you just met," she said, "is not the Czar I remember."

"You left a long time ago," I said. Hadn't she?

"I did," she said. "But Yure Danko has been leader of the Black Souls for most of my life and I have a very good memory." She ran her hands through her golden hair. "The brilliant sorcerer I knew, the dangerous man, is gone." She shook her head. "I wasn't told he'd begun to lose his mind and I'd like to know why."

"I'll come with you." It was clear she had somewhere else to be, likely somewhere I might find answers about Charlotte.

Isabelle stepped away, shaking her head in a tight motion, eyes sparking with white flame. "This I must do alone," she said. "But I will return, Sydlynn Hayle. With the information we seek."

She shuddered into shadow and vanished before I could grab her. My lunge as she shifted to darkness sent me through the place she'd been and forward, stumbling into a chair. Where I swore. For a long time, swear words I'd learned from friends, from enemies, on and on in a vile string until I clenched my hands into fists and let out a tight shriek.

Are you finished? My vampire sighed. *Really, Sydlynn.*

Leave her alone, my demon sent. *I have a few more for you to try out, if you want.*

I could feel Shaylee blushing. Sighed myself as I turned and sank into the chair I'd almost fallen over, shoulders slumping as I collapsed into the seat.

Sorry. Wasn't really. But the response was automatic.

So, what now? Shaylee's voice quivered. *We can't just leave her there.*

We're not, I snapped. Cooled off again. *But if Gwendolyn and Finlay can free her…*

They would have already, my demon growled.

We wait, my vampire sent, the voice of undead reason. *A war between territories will only feed the needs of the Brotherhood. And while we all know Applegate is under their control, if there is a way to defeat her without bringing hardship, we need to take that path.*

First Charlotte, I sent. *And then we deal with Applegate.* This couldn't go on any longer. Not while witches in Europe knew full well what was happening and no one acted.

Agreed. Three egos hugged me, the family magic rising to swirl around us while the sorcery beneath me shivered with the need to feed.

We'll give them twenty-four hours, I sent. *Then we go get Charlotte and to hell with Applegate.*

Murmurs of acceptance. I thudded both fists down on the arms of the chair, so hard I almost missed the knock on my door.

I know I was supposed to be nice and everything, but visiting hours were over, thanks. I strode to the door to banish whoever was behind it, jerking it wide just as a wave of black crashed over me. My alter egos gasped even as the black blossom of my sorcery opened, but too late.

The darkness washed over me as my anger burned, crackling with irritation I'd fallen into a trap.

chapter fourteen

I came out of the dark as angry as I went in. It felt like swimming to the surface of a boiling lake, freezing cold beneath, flaming hot at the top. My demon practically leaped from my body when we surfaced into consciousness, pulling me upright, amber fire scorching the air around me.

Surrounded, blackness everywhere, the hum of werewolf energy, the pooling dark of sorcery. Yure Danko obviously had more he wanted to say to me.

And I had so much more to tell him. Though I would let my actions speak.

Let's see what a long, painful death did for his sense of godhood.

"Please, wait." My eyes tried to focus, heart pounding in time with my demon's pants, my vampire's hissing loud in my head even as the ground beneath me rumbled,

Shaylee sharing her unhappiness. "We're not your enemies."

What a load of—

Hang on. No one attacked. In fact, I felt magic retreating. No way would the so-called Czar and his people give me the chance to get my feet under me, to shake the delirium of the black from my head. I staggered upright, the family magic begging to be released even as I smothered it further. If this was a trick, some means to make me use my power and give Applegate a reason to ban me from Europe, I wasn't taking the bait.

Not yet, anyway.

And it wasn't just dark because I was having trouble with my vision. Wherever I now found myself, there was very little light. My reaching hands, searching for support, met flesh, strong fingers, a powerful grip, firm but gentle. His sorcery connected with mine, but that was all. Just a touch to let me know he was there.

I turned, my eyes finding the moon outside a cracked and filthy window, teeth chattering all over again as shock and the cold set in. My demon sniffed around this stranger, not sure if she believed him friend or foe. I almost pushed him away, but the moment I moved to free myself my knees buckled and it was only his arm around my waist keeping me from going down.

"I'm sorry." His voice was low, a soft British accent not nearly as noticeable as Gwendolyn's adding a lilt to

115

his voice. "We wanted to be sure you didn't give us trouble before we made it out of town. Are you all right?"

My vampire's spirit magic raced through me, burning away the last traces of whatever drug they'd used to knock me out. The flare of sorcery of the initial attack had clearly only been a way to distract me so the drug could take effect. So noted for the future.

Spirit power sizzled in my veins, waking me the rest of the way. I became acutely aware of the way this body felt against mine, the subtle scents of coffee and mint. Even in the low light coming through the windows, I made out his features as he looked down at me.

Damn it, why were all the cute ones so tall? Long blonde hair hung over one of his shoulders, his perfectly arched eyebrows raised over large eyes pale in the moonlight. High cheekbones framed his angled face, mouth a tense line as he gently let me go. I shivered, hugging myself, my wool pea coat no match for the freezing night air.

"You'd better have a damned good explanation for kidnapping me," I said, letting my demon out to growl while Shaylee shook the ground again. "If I don't hear something I like in five seconds, I'm not taking any prisoners. So start talking."

My captor shrugged his wide shoulders, floor-length greatcoat reminding me of Kristophe and his stupid wardrobe. Only on this guy, it looked great.

Damn it.

"I'm more than happy to do so," he said, bowing a little. "But I'm afraid it will have to wait." He glanced out the window with a tight expression before turning back to me. "We didn't make it nearly as far as I'd hoped before you began to wake." Was that admiration in his voice? "If we are to steal away to a safe location, we need to leave immediately."

"And what," I stiffened, fighting the cold for control, "makes you think," teeth chattering did nothing for my tough-girl act, "I'm going anywhere with you?"

"Because, Sydlynn," he said, offering his hand again. "I'm the only person who can help you free Charlotte Girard."

Someone eased closer, a shadow in the dark. When he turned his face, the moonlight touching familiar features, I sagged into the truth. Raoul looked back at me, misery in his eyes, the former wereguard of the Dumont family—Charlotte's father—looking as upset as I felt.

"I beg you," he said. "For my daughter, if she was ever your friend, as she claims. Trust these sorcerers. They are her only hope."

I hadn't seen Raoul since he abandoned me, just after Mom was arrested. Ran like a scared rabbit, leaving his daughter to pick up his slack. So much for werewolf honor. And yet, looking at me with his mix of worry and guilt added a thin layer to my growing trust.

Fine. I'd follow along with sorcerer boy. Until tall, blonde and yummynom proved to be either a liar or a major pain in my backside. The second he proved to be a liability or a threat, I'd be kicking his handsome ass.

Two other sorcerers and a handful of werewolves moved closer, guiding us out the back of the abandoned house and into a waiting truck. The rusted thing looked like the 70s called and wanted their beat-up disaster back. I was hustled into the truck bed with a boost from cutie patootie I really didn't need. And was he just looking at my ass?

Boys.

Turned out they got me under the cover of the makeshift tarp just in time. Empty-feeling power rolled over me, shielding and disguising me as a pair of blue flame flares burst into view overhead. I held my breath, knew the Enforcers had to be looking for me. Word of my kidnapping wouldn't have made it far past Applegate's awareness. And the idea I was out here, somewhere, unsupervised had to be yanking her chain.

This was the moment. If I wanted to be rescued, get away from Raoul and whatever his sorcerer friends were up to, all I had to do was say the word. Not that they were a threat. I wasn't getting threatening vibes from scrumptiouspants who hovered next to me, cheek practically pressed to mine as we shared the view. But I wasn't sure I was really interested in their agenda, aside from my need to get Charlotte back.

The only reason I didn't cut and run.

Not like me to take the easy route anyway. I held still, waiting, watched the black-robed forms float overhead through the back window and out the windshield of the old truck before the same blue fire flashed and they were gone.

Sorcerer boy grinned at me, winked as he withdrew his protective black shield. Kissed my cold cheek with his warm lips, a little flare of flame waking my skin. "Thank you," he said. "Now, if you'd like to take the place of honor," he gestured with exaggerated aplomb at a ratty old car seat tucked in the front corner of the truck bed, "we have places to be."

Well, since he put it that way.

CHAPTER FIFTEEN

Someone fired up the engine, the truck coughing once into the night before roaring to life. I heard others doing the same around us as I settled into the sagging seat jerry-rigged to the covered bed of the truck. My companion perched beside me on the curve of metal over the back wheel, thigh pressed to mine, one arm around the back of my seat while Raoul crouched, in perfect balance despite the roughness of the ride, his eyes glowing in wolfish intensity as the beast within him kept him stable.

"You're wondering who we are," Blondie said as casually as though we sat over a cup of coffee, not bouncing our way down a rutted track through the dark forest in a rattling death trap so loud he had to almost shout to be heard. I peeked out the open back, missing the light of the moon, even as a pair of headlights flared to life right in my eyes from a following vehicle. I looked away, squinting, catching the smile on the young sorcerer's face, the speculation.

The nearness of his lips.

Wanted to smack him for the sultry heat in his grin.

What was it with me and the boys who took me captive? My demon friend, Rameranselot, and I met the same way. And even though I knew we'd never be a couple, he was still smoking hot.

Not going to think that way this time.

Not.

"What gave it away?" Ah, sarcasm. The last refuge of my need for protective irritation.

He laughed, leaned in further, stretching his long legs out in front of him while I huddled and shivered and wished he'd put his arm around me rather than the back of the seat.

For. Warmth.

Sigh.

"My name is Piers Southway," he said. "And I'm with the Steam Union."

The—

"About time you guys decided to pull your hands out of your butts and take action." Wow, I really hadn't meant to be such a bitch, honest. But all the frustration of dealing not only with Yure but the Brotherhood for all this time without help or a sniff of interest from the so-called good guy sorcerers surged to the surface in a wave of temper catching me off- guard. My demon hit him hard in the chest with a fist of fire while my vampire slammed him back against the side of the truck.

Shaylee wanted to help, but I figured shaking the ground while we were in a moving vehicle in as bad a shape as this one might be a risky idea.

Raoul didn't react to the attack, except to bare his teeth in what looked like a nasty smile. So, I wasn't the only one to think the Steam Union dropped the very large spherical object, was that it?

Piers gasped for a breath, but, to his credit, he didn't fight me. Just kept his gaze level and soft as he fought for air.

"—not—my—fault." His eyes were beginning to bulge a little.

"Of course it's not." I smiled sweetly as my vampire tightened her hold, a waft of smoke rising from his jacket where my demon pinned him still. "It's never anyone's fault, is it?" I glanced at the silent, grinning werewolf. "What do you think, Raoul?" I sat back, my anger giving me the warmth I needed to speak without my teeth clacking together. "Buying it?"

More fang, a soft growl, shake of a head.

Yeah. Me either.

I let Piers go anyway, if only to avoid having an unconscious body to deal with. Or a dead one for that matter. Besides, he was right about me wanting answers and, at the moment, he was my only option.

"Okay, sorcerer boy," I said. "Spill your guts."

He drew three deep breaths before he could speak. "Trust me," he said at last, "I've been as eager to act against the Brotherhood as you. In fact, I've been lobbying to offer you aid for almost a year now."

So he said. The sincerity in his voice, the way he leaned toward me again despite what I just did to him, gave him at least enough credibility I didn't let my demon heave him out the back.

Yet.

"I take it your people had a breakthrough in their little moral dilemma to let me deal with their mess." Okay, my mess, too. But still. They were sorcerers, supposed to be the good guys, if Gram and Demetrius were to be believed. And I'd been acting alone for so long, without support, it was hard to just let go of my animosity.

"I convinced them to act," Piers said. "On your behalf. And on ours." He sighed, shrugged. "My people fear we are too weak to stand against our dark brothers. But your arrival, the rise of the maji and the coming of the prophecy, has finally convinced them we can't be complacent." He took my cold hands in his and warmed them. How was it he was so very warm and I was slowly turning into a Sydscicle?

"You're the reason we're here," he said, leaning over me, pale eyes intense. "The catalyst. But if we are to act as a people, it must ultimately be for our own good. So I thank you for giving us the impetus to take a stand where once we hid in shadow."

Well. If nothing else, he talked pretty. Sure did.

The truck slowed, gears grinding as we turned from the forest path onto a narrow lane. Snow began to fall, shining in the glaring headlights behind us as the engine roared before we slid to a halt. Piers almost ended up in my lap even while Raoul's balance wasn't affected.

Made me think of Charlotte. Miss her all the more.

"There are further answers waiting for you inside." Piers stood as the truck went quiet, the sound of doors opening and slamming closed following as the other two vehicles halted around us. He crouched under the short canopy of the tarp covering the back of the truck. His offered hand beckoned, small smile curving his mouth, blonde hair spilling over the dark fabric of his coat, the scent of him stronger now for some reason. My demon breathed it in and, for the first time since we met him, hummed happily. A familiar sound I'd only ever heard her hum with one other person.

Oh no, she did *not*.

She lifted my hand for me, reaching to him, the warmth of the memory of his skin on mine enticing if only because I was freezing.

Yeah, that was it. I was just cold and he wasn't.

Syd. Seriously.

Before my demon could reconnect our grip, I stood on my own, pushing past Piers, slipping out the back and into the snow. I was immediately doused in a fall of soft flakes, reminding me of Harvard and what I'd left behind only a few short hours ago.

The weekend seemed like it was years away.

And Liam.

Oh dear.

Time to focus on Charlotte and get my ass home before I could add another complication to my list of hot guys I really needed to avoid.

chapter sixteen

The large, stone house looked like someone's ancestral farm, just this side of an estate, really, outbuildings and fences leading off into the darkness. A single light burned over the red-painted front door. I followed Piers as he led the way, others closing in around me from the other two vehicles. The faces of the sorcerers Piers brought with him were young, two girls, two guys, though the werewolves were all older and few in number, considering the horde I'd met at Yure's palace.

Outnumbered and outgunned? Story of my life.

The warm interior hit me like a blow, hot air almost as big a shock to my system as the drug they'd used to subdue me. The place smelled of wood smoke and meat, my stomach growling at the latter.

Oppressive dark-paneled walls pushed down on me as I walked the narrow hall, a few doors on either side closed to view. My hands clenched in my pockets as we turned through the last doorway at the end of the corridor and into a large study.

A massive fire blazed in a gaping fireplace on the far wall, pumping heat into the air. I hated to judge, but there was a distinct scent of wet dog fur mixed with the smoke and bite of pipe tobacco.

But it wasn't the smell I cared about. A huge man stood, his back to me, hands clasped behind him, staring down into the flames rising from the huge logs burning steadily in the hearth. Shaggy silver hair glinted in the light as Raoul stepped past me and went to him. I glanced around the room, noting the werewolves, both male and female, gathered to watch me with glowing eyes, only two small lamps with solid flames and the fire itself for illumination.

Younger weres, mixed with older, all sharing similar features. Charlotte's family, I guessed. I could see her eyes in some of the women, though their sad, weary faces were nothing like the Charlotte I held firmly in my mind.

I was not going to think about the weregirl I'd just seen.

Not when I planned to get the old Charlotte back.

The large man bent his body sideways as Raoul, a head shorter, leaned in. One of his hands settled on the older were's shoulder, lips near his ear, an air of comfortable familiarity between them. Beads of sweat popped out on my upper lip as the heat melted the snow in my hair, pulling the strength from me. My demon loved it, but such a switch in temperature was making me feel woozy.

The big were nodded to Raoul, turned to grip his face in his hands, kiss both cheeks before facing me. More glowing wolf eyes as he strode toward me, massive hands reaching for mine, weathered face kind behind a thick silver beard and mustache.

"Forgive us," he said in almost perfect English, accented British, only a hint of his Ukrainian heritage behind his words. "This was the only way."

I could see Charlotte in his features, way more than her father. "You could have asked."

He nodded. "And yet, had we, you would have been forced to lie about your meeting with us. This way, if Margaret Applegate asks you if you were kidnapped, she will have no recourse but to believe you."

Clever. Still a sucky way to try to make a friend. But I'd let it pass.

"I am Oleksander Moreau," he said in his gravelly bass voice, pressing one hand to his wide chest. No matter the deep wrinkles on his face, the thick hair on his head as silver as his beard, I had no doubt age had done nothing to sap his strength. I felt it emanating from him, the power, the way his big hand squeezed mine with a gentle touch. So much crushing power behind it I knew even with magic I'd be hard-pressed to keep my bones intact if he decided to squeeze. "Sharlotta—ah forgive me, Charlotte," his accent bit off her Americanized name abruptly, "is my granddaughter."

"Sydlynn Hayle." I shrugged. "She's my friend."

His eyes flared once before settling into the same blue as Charlotte's. "From what I understand," he said, "we have you to thank for her survival."

"Trust me," I said, feeling myself relax at the pinched expression on his face, the way his concern rolled over me, "I was only returning the favor."

His smile shone like a beacon. "Our Sharlotta has a fire inside her I wish I could capture and share with all of our people." He led me further into the room, guided me to a wide-backed seat with a deep cushion, helping me personally with my coat. The wool shed, I felt instantly better, the room hot enough even my t-shirt and jeans were almost too much. "We are very proud of her."

Choke. I blinked a couple of times to still the sting in my eyes. "Ditto."

Oleksander sat himself, tree-trunk thighs crushing the cushion beneath him, forearms almost as wide as his hands resting on the faded velvet. His blue eyes never left me as he clutched the ends of the armrests with his giant fingers. "You know by now who she is to our people."

I nodded, glanced at Raoul. "I take it you're her maternal grandfather?"

"I am," he said. "Charlotte chose to take another surname, Girard, when she was forced into servitude with the Dumonts. She didn't want the Moreau family name sullied by their evil." He bowed his head, firelight creating shadows across the grooved wrinkles on his cheek. Raoul twitched, head ducking as Oleksander went on. "She is the best and bravest of us. I could not ask for a more noble grandchild."

"Where is Charlotte's mother?" He opened the door to personal, and I took it. All the questions I'd ever had about my werefriend came rushing to the surface. While Charlotte might not have been willing to spill her guts, Oleksander didn't seem to have the same reserve. I tried not to feel badly she probably would have hated the fact he was telling me so much she'd managed to keep secret.

But on the other hand, sucked to be her.

"Lost to us," he said, pain in his voice. "Olena died defending our family from the Czar. Our dear Charlotte and her brother, Danilo, witnessed their mother's death at his hands, still defiant and fighting, giving the children enough time to flee. According to Danilo, he had to drag Charlotte away." He smiled sadly, moisture glistening in his eyes. "Even at the tender age of seven, she was a warrior at heart."

Okay, damn it, how could I hold back my own tears? I did, barely, jaw working as I fought to keep my throat from closing.

"What is she doing back here?" I wanted to choke her all of a sudden. "Why did she put herself in a position where she could be captured?" She was smarter than that, or, at least, I thought she was.

And why the hell didn't she come to me for help?

"She was lured into returning," Raoul spoke up, grief and guilt in his voice, his accent much heavier than Oleksander's. "And it's my fault she's now captive."

The old were raised one hand, shaking his head. "Not true," Oleksander said. "We will not blame our people for honor bred into us since our conception. We will, instead, focus our fury at those who made us and continue to try to use us for their gain."

I liked him even more than I had when we first met. "She just left." Misery rose in my heart, made it even harder not to cry. I felt a single tear escape, swiped at it quickly. "I would have helped her if she'd just come to me."

Oleksander leaned forward, patted my knee with a sad smile. "Pride is our greatest weakness," he said. "She would never have asked for your aid."

"The Czar knew about you," Raoul said, resentment and anger replacing his regret. "About your bond."

"He did, indeed." Oleksander sat back, elbows on the armrests as he steepled his hands before him. "He has been trying for centuries to break our spirit, Sydlynn. But our family has stood firm against him, despite our forced servitude."

"You're free now." I looked around me at the gathered werewolves, felt their sadness squeeze me tight.

"Not so." Oleksander sighed, a gusty sound over the crackling of the fire. "Though he owns our souls, he has never broken our spirits like those of our lesser brothers and sisters." Full of himself much? The old werewolf pursed his lips, mustache quivering. "Who are we to understand the mind of a madman? We are well aware he could crush us at any moment." Okay, so not as arrogant as I thought. I cut him some slack as he went on. "I suppose it is a tactic he employs to control the rest of our kind. Knowing we have some freedoms keeps the others in check." Oleksander shifted in his seat, clearly uncomfortable with the admission of his own weakness. "The Czar has simply allowed us to live apart, giving the remainder of our people false hope we may someday rise up against him. Though, at least, he does not dare kill us, at risk of creating martyrs."

"Or whispers of an heir's survival," Raoul said. "Such as those of the Romanov's when he had them slain."

"We do what we can," Oleksander said, "but we are still his slaves. And when he calls, we must obey."

I prodded my pain like an aching tooth. "So you all knew about the bond, too, I take it."

Oleksander dropped his hands, solid thuds vibrating his chair. "We did," he said. "We've been watching her.

When she took her father's place," not a whisper of judgment, though the other werewolves shifted uneasily and Raoul's head hung in shame, "we were proud to know our favorite child was bonded to such a powerful personage as yourself." Oleksander's smile made my chest ache in guilt. "We had thought her safe with you. It was my hope she would remain in America as your wereguard and not be drawn back into our family curse. The Czar would not be able to touch her, not without invoking your wrath. At least one of us, the best of us, would be safe."

I coughed softly to loosen the regret holding my throat in spasm. "I had no idea," I said. "When she almost died, I didn't know the bond was broken."

"Nor did we," he said. "There is no way of knowing. But Charlotte knew." He paused before going on. "She telephoned me several months after it happened, furious, terrified. Told me what had happened. She was distraught. I begged her to talk to you, for by then your reputation had preceded you, your own honor as powerful as ours, I believed." He continued to smile. "Still believe. But she refused."

Idiot weregirl. When I finally rescued her, she'd better look the hell out.

"Without the bond to hold her," Oleksander said, "when the Czar called, Charlotte had no choice."

chapter seventeen

Quiet settled over the room, the air so thick with oppression my chest felt tight.

"My friend, Galleytrot, was able to free Raoul." I met the werewolf's eyes. "And Charlotte and some of her friends. I know he can help the rest of you."

Oleksander nodded, sitting forward again, hunger flaring in the wolf that rose to his face for a moment. A grizzled muzzle and fiery eyes transformed him from a man to a were and back again. "He did, you are correct. But the bond he destroyed was the one to the Dumont family. We are still created from the sorcerers, and once the Czar had possession of Raoul and the others again, he was able to reestablish his hold."

"Is it like the bond?" I really had no freaking clue. But if I could free them all permanently, I would.

"No," Oleksander said. "The bond is something

entirely different. Done on purpose, with purpose, by the werewolf to one he or she chooses to protect out of love or duty." He growled softly under his breath in Ukrainian before going on. "The hold Yure Danko has over us, the Black Souls, comes from our very creation."

There has to be a way. I ducked inside, addressed the girls.

Agreed, my vampire sent. *But it might require maji power, Sydlynn. Power you don't have access to right now.*

To hell with Applegate. My demon's rage bit through the conversation in a flare of flame. *These people have suffered long enough with this asshat.*

Shaylee sighed. *It's possible. But I believe we will need Galleytrot's guidance to tell us what he did, exactly.*

Oleksander must have known I was gone from him because one hand gently touched mine, regaining my attention. "The Czar has done everything he can to break us over the years, from public beatings to selling us to a certain witch family to prove our weakness." The Dumonts. Right. They had to have been in league with Yure or, at least, knew him well enough he understood their twisted coven would be the perfect choice. "But my grandson, Danilo, managed to escape. Pushed past the boundaries the Czar has allowed us to live inside." Pride shone in his eyes, sadness in his voice. "He had been working with other witches, searching for help. He even went to the Steam Union," Oleksander glanced at Piers, "and brought us a message of hope."

"Danilo was my friend," Piers said, voice soft, thick.

Was. "The Czar killed him." The only explanation for their sudden grief.

Oleksander's face twisted, one hand fisting in front of his mouth as he turned his head away a moment. "Shortly after Charlotte's near death, her brother was murdered."

"Did she know?" My heart skipped, clenched. I thought of Meira and what I would do if someone hurt her. Rage and grief bubbled for Charlotte as Raoul stared into the fire, face lit orange as he answered my question.

"She did," he said. "When she appealed to me for help about her bond with you, I was forced to tell her."

How had she stayed with me for so long, not told me, knowing her own brother was dead at the hands of her enemy…? And yet, the weird behavior I though tied to the loss of our bond, the way she was always so short with me, how she acted when I found out I was supposed to marry by twenty-one. All of it fit together like a sick and tragic puzzle. And now I knew, I thought back, realized just how unhappy she was, how tense, withdrawn even more than I was used to. How angry.

Not at me.

Oh, Charlotte.

I wept then, unable to hold in my tears, hands over my mouth to keep control of my sobs. Oleksander's big hand squeezed my knee again as I pulled myself under control.

Yure Danko was a dead man.

"With Danilo's loss," Oleksander said, voice thick, "Charlotte became the prime focus of the Czar's attention. I am old." He shook his head. "And while I am the leading member of our family, it is Charlotte who represents the future of our people." The whole room sighed as the werewolves gathered shifted as one, exhaling their thin hope. "When the Czar looked for Charlotte and found she bonded to you, he became enraged. It is his intention to marry her, his final act of degradation. To turn her not only into his slave, but his forced bride, to finally crush the last of our family pride into dust with her wedded enslavement. I shudder to consider what abominations she might bear him."

"Charlotte would not allow that to happen," Raoul said. "She would end her own life, first."

Holy. Crap. "No one is ending anything," I snarled at her father. "And Charlotte is not, under any circumstances, marrying that nasty piece of work." I fixed Oleksander with a scowl. "I promise you that."

He bobbed a nod, wiping at his own wet cheeks. "I knew she had a faithful friend in you, Sydlynn," he said. "I had to believe it."

Yeah, he'd better.

The whole Yure Danko was a dead man? Times that by a million and throw in some creative demon torture and a Sidhe earth stomping while he burned forever in the white flames of vampire fury.

"The Czar sent Charlotte Danilo's bones," Oleksander said. I shuddered. Witch bones were sacred, the last connection to their magic, their echoes. Were werewolf remains the same? "To taunt her. Claimed he had Raoul in his clutches."

"Which wasn't true." Charlotte's father trembled, hands clenched at his sides, punching his own thighs in a steady rhythm.

"She didn't know," Oleksander said, tone soothing. "When she tried to reach both of us, Yure blocked her at every turn. And so she returned when Yure said he would do the same to her father as he did to Danilo if she did not accept his offer."

I could only imagine the war going on inside Charlotte, her need to protect me, her grief for her lost mother and brother, her fear for one of her only remaining family members. Of course she would do the right thing and choose her biological family.

I would expect nothing less of her. But, damn her. I could have helped.

"It is our belief," Piers said, standing from his perch on the arm of the sofa, coming to stand next to Raoul, "the Czar believed Charlotte was still bonded to you. Luring her here would mean capturing you at the same time."

I flashed a snarl at Piers. Wished that had been the case.

"He would have had a bit of a shock, I'm thinking." I let my demon play out a scenario in my mind, one where the over-done palace lay in rubble on the snowy ground and the arrogant and deluded Danko pleaded for mercy at my feet.

Piers laughed. "I think you're right. And he still might."

"When the Czar discovered Charlotte was alone, the bond broken, he insisted she agree to his terms." Oleksander shifted in his chair, anger rising, a living thing, feeding the fury of the gathered werewolves. "Back in his clutches and forced to bond to him personally, she had created her own trap."

"Out of options, her soul sold to save me," Raoul grimaced as though he wished she'd let him die, "she did the only thing she could do."

Oleksander nodded sadly. "She kept her honor. And her word. To an honor-less man who doesn't deserve her."

Damn it, Charlotte.

Werewolf sensibilities were going to get me into a lot of trouble.

chapter eighteen

The air beside Piers shuddered with shadow only a moment before Isabelle appeared. I almost jumped out of my seat, a meep of shock escaping at her sudden arrival and, for a heartbeat, I was afraid the gig was up and Gwendolyn and Finlay would arrive right behind her.

But the lack of werewolf reaction to her appearance, the way Oleksander greeted the vampire with a nod of welcome, made my stomach squirm with suspicion.

"You've been working with them all along." Came out as an accusation and I meant it as one.

Isabelle nodded, biting her bottom lip. "I'm sorry, Sydlynn," she said. "I'm the reason the werewolves and Steam Union knew where to find you."

"Sunny will be thrilled to know you're not faithful to your blood clan." Not fair, really. After all, this bunch proved themselves trustworthy, at least so far. And we had the same goal, to free Charlotte. But my jab had the desired effect, Isabelle's face crumpling in upset as she wrung her slim, white hands.

"I swear that's not true." She came to kneel beside me, gripping the arm of my chair with tight fingers. "My blood clan is my life. But." She glanced at Oleksander. "I love a werewolf being held by the Czar and it is my goal to free him." Isabelle's cheeks glistened with tears. "And I knew if anyone could do so, it would be you."

Seemed my reputation was getting around all right. And inviting more trouble.

"Please, do not blame dear Isabelle." Oleksander stroked the girl's hair. "She has been a friend of the Moreau family for centuries, served the true Czars. She has done everything in her power to help and protect us from her father."

Isabelle twitched while alarm bells went off in my head. "What little power I have." She said.

"Father?" Oh, tell me I was wrong, that she hadn't convinced Shaylee to hide her and put us all in danger because—

"It's true," Isabelle's shoulders sagged. "Yure Danko is my father."

My teeth ground together, the sound so loud I had to force myself to stop before I powdered what was left of my molars.

"And you didn't think it was a good idea to let me

know we were walking you into the lion's den?" She was so close smacking her would have been simple.

"He would have done nothing to me," she said. "But I knew if he saw me with you he would use both Charlotte and you against me." She turned away, still kneeling, rubbing her arms as though cold though there was no way anyone could feel a chill in this room. "My father has hated me since I fled after the deaths of the Romanovs and my crossing to the undead. He considers me a traitor and will do anything to make me suffer."

"Including hurt your werewolf boyfriend." So she wanted to hide for him, not really for me. Well, at least now I understood her motivations. "You just came with me so you could see lover boy."

Isabelle shook her head, faced me again, eyes huge and full of sincerity. What was with these people and their openness? Didn't they realize they should hold something back?

"No," she said. "My only thought was for Charlotte. And you. I swear it."

I told my inner bitch to back off a second and laid my head on the padded wingback.

"Hang on," I said. "How can you have a were boyfriend?" I looked up to meet Oleksander's eyes. "I thought vampires couldn't stand werewolves." At least, according to Sunny.

"I grew up around them as a human girl," Isabelle

said, drawing my attention back to her. "When I became a vampire, it took some time, but I was able to adjust to the feeling of our opposing magicks." Her eyes shone with the bubbly, empty-headed adoration of young love.

Cynic.

"And when I met Maksym," she went on, voice practically throbbing with emotion, "I knew I had to find a way to finally free the werewolves from my father's grasp forever."

"The Rusak family, Maksym's line, has been our faithful supporter all along," Oleksander said. "Doing what they can from inside the ranks of those serving the Black Souls. Maksym is no exception."

"But he is." Isabelle turned on Oleksander, now clinging to his big knee. "He told me the Czar was as powerful as ever, that nothing had changed." She wept, burying her face in her hands. "But I have seen my father, great wolf, and he is not the sorcerer he used to be."

Oleksander's scowl pulled at his rugged features. "What are you talking about?"

"I'm with Isabelle," I said. "Whoever is pulling the strings over at the palace, it isn't Yure Danko."

Oleksander sat back with a loud sigh, eyes narrowing as his beard bristled aggressively. "This must be Vasyl's doing."

Interesting. "He claimed he was the security head, but I get the impression he's more than that."

Raoul growled, the sound of unhappy werewolves echoing him as the whole room shifted.

"He rose in ranks a year ago," Oleksander said. "He was nothing but a minor power until that time. And then, he was at the Czar's side, whispering in his ear."

"This we knew," Isabelle said. "But now that I've seen the Czar, how weak and deluded he's become, I can only guess as well it's someone's doing. And Vasyl does seem the logical choice."

Were they serious? Had they been ignoring what was happening in the magic world around them? This whole situation smacked of interference, all right.

And I was pretty sure I knew exactly whose fingers tainted this particular pie.

"The Brotherhood." I slammed my fist down on the armrest, my demon snarling behind my voice.

Oleksander looked startled, Isabelle gasping in shock. Even Piers frowned before swearing softly and turning away from me, head down.

"Seriously?" I looked around at the eyes staring at me. "You didn't expect Liander Belaisle to find a way to worm his way in?"

Oleksander said something in Ukrainian, the wolf returning to his face. "We did not," he said. "But your suggestion has weight."

"Danilo died just as Charlotte and I were fighting the Brotherhood." Damn it, Belaisle had to have already had his act in place with the Czar and his Black Souls. How did the man stay so many steps ahead of me and how could I possibly anticipate what he would do next? "Why didn't the Czar kill Danilo years ago if he was stirring up trouble?"

No one spoke, just stared at me, mute.

"Because the Czar didn't want him dead. But the Brotherhood did." So clear, crystal, bright and terrible. "They wanted Charlotte." To get to me. "Used her dead brother against her." To get to me. "And now, they are forcing her to marry a man they've manipulated and likely control."

To get to me.

Deep-fried hate wrapped in a red-hot tortilla.

"This hasn't been about your family." I surged to my feet, found the room packed as I tried to pace. Forced myself to stand still as my brain churned. "It's about the war that's coming. Another move on the chess board."

How many people would fall in the crossfire before this was over?

Isabelle sobbed once before rising and taking my hands. Hers were freezing. She'd clearly not eaten, the skin transparent as she clutched at me.

"No matter the truth," she said, voice barely above a whisper. "We must act." She looked to Oleksander, still holding on to me. "And soon. I may have betrayed us all by speaking with Maksym."

The gathered weres and sorcerers all gasped, whispered, tension in the room rising. I squeezed Isabelle's hand before pulling free of her.

"We need to change our plans." Oleksander rose as well, turning to Piers. The young sorcerer looked worried, grim. His gray eyes skimmed over me and to the hulking werewolf leader. "If the Brotherhood truly holds the reins, everything has changed."

Piers's head bobbed in a dejected nod. "No matter my best intentions," he said, "even I know my people aren't strong enough to take on the Brotherhood." His eyes met mine. "Danilo convinced me to help his people against the Czar and his small group of sorcerers. But the Brotherhood's involvement is a game-changer."

I almost prodded him, resentment toward Belaisle and his people bubbling, making me cranky. How could Piers have missed this?

Because, my vampire sent in her soft, steady voice, *he is young and ambitious and just wants to do the right thing.*

Jumped before he thought about it out of loyalty or something, my demon sent, words heavy with sarcasm. *Sound familiar?*

Shaylee's giggle just made me snarl.

I left the werewolves and sorcerers, walking out into the hall, and not one person tried to stop me. Three doors down, I found a bedroom and sank onto the hand-made quilt, hugging myself in the dark. The room was cool after the oppressive heat of the study, but enough warmth reached it from the raging fire I adjusted quickly.

Wasn't really thinking about my physical comfort, anyway. Not while I fought to grasp the goals of the Brotherhood.

One thing was certain, I needed to talk to someone and there wasn't a soul here who could give me the insight I needed. As much as I hated risking alerting Applegate to my location, I had to. Besides, Mom would be worried.

I opened myself to my mother, shielding heavily with sorcery, letting the thinnest thread of witch magic travel from me to her.

Syd! She grasped onto me with a bear hug, her power surging toward me before I blocked her with my vampire magic. Her mind and magic hovered, shaking with anxiety, at the border to the European territory.

Mom, I'm fine. I showed her where I was, that I was safe. Only then did she back off. I followed her mind on the return trip, found her in her office chair. Well, standing half out of it, face clenched in fear.

Margaret. Mom's mind gasped. *She told me you were kidnapped. That she was searching for you.* Mom settled, body relaxing as she breathed, our connection so strong I felt her hands unclench from the edge of her desk as she settled in her seat. *She wouldn't let me come to help.*

How many times had I done what I now did, giving her the run-down on the disaster I'd found myself a part of? As usual, Mom listened in silence, absorbing what I had to say. But this Mom was totally herself, the woman who raised me, loved me, without the touch of the Brotherhood to keep her from hearing all of it.

Mom. I drew a breath, letting it out in a long, slow exhale. *What should I do?* It felt so weird, having to ask. Usually I just acted, didn't give a crap about the consequences. But she and the Council had given me a massive responsibility when they'd granted me the power to act on their behalf. And I'd finally begun to accept the full weight of what that power meant. One false move and I could start a war that would put all of us in the hands of the Brotherhood.

Coven Leader Hayle. Mom's mental voice crackled in my mind. *I thought I told you already, but allow me to repeat myself for clarity. Save Charlotte. And let me deal with Margaret Applegate.*

I love you, Mom. I sagged where I sat, arms falling free, hands loose in my lap.

I love you, too, she said. *Just do it quickly and quietly.*

You betcha. I hesitated. Could I just lift Charlotte from the Czar and leave her people to suffer? Would she let me? Hell, would I let me?

Having an overactive sense of fair play sucked sometimes.

What about the werewolves, Mom?

She sighed, shook her head. *Sweetheart... they aren't our*

problem. I could hear the regret in her mental voice, feel the pain it caused her to say those words. *They are on their own.* She paused again. *For now.*

I hated to agree with her. But she was right.

Charlotte it was. As long as my werefriend would allow me rescue her.

I let Mom go, starting as the door creaked open. There was enough moonlight coming through the window I recognized Raoul's face as he entered, head bowed.

He knelt at my feet before I could stop him. "She has more *can* than I ever will," he said, tears in his voice. "My daughter brings me great pride—and accentuates my own shame." He looked up, met my eyes. "Your kindness freed us from the Dumonts. And I will never forget the sacrifice your family was asked to make to do so." Uncle Frank almost died, burned by the sun. Did I blame the werewolves? Maybe a little then, for guarding the wretched Dumonts. But not now I understood they had no choice. "I should have stood by you when Miriam was on trial." He shook as he reached out to touch my knee with one hand. "But I feared for my people, so newly freed. I took the coward's way and I will always, always, regret my decision." His shoulders twitched. "It is your place, as the one I've wronged, to decide my fate."

Um, what?

"Though my people would never say it, I know they

judge me for leaving you behind." Raoul's voice dropped to a whisper. "It was only Charlotte's bond with you that saved my *сан*."

"It's okay," I said. Weak, Hayle. But what else was I going to say?

"It isn't." He bowed his head even lower. "My life is in your hands, Coven Leader Hayle. To do with as you see fit."

Oh boy.

Before I could act, speak, Raoul offered his hand. "You may kill me," he said, voice toneless, dead. "Or you can demand I become your *пов'язаний*. That choice is yours."

I shoved him away, temper on fire suddenly, threaded through by the grief of what his people's honor had done to them. My feet scuffed over the floorboards as I stood over him, my demon writhing in anger.

"Listen up," I snapped. "You are your own person. I don't own you, you don't owe me anything. I tried to get that message through the hard head of your very stubborn daughter, and I failed. But I'll be damned if I don't get through to you."

His head snapped up part way through my speech and gaped at me.

"I don't want your death," I said. "Or your bond. It's not about having a bodywere, you idiot. It's about caring about someone enough you'll do anything for them, no strings attached." I turned away from him, stormed to the door as Piers peeked his head in, eyebrows raised. I turned back to Raoul who stared after me, face sad. "It's time you and the other werewolves understood that."

I joined Piers in the hall, a little bit out of breath I felt so angry.

"Are you all right?" His little smile nearly set me off again, though the touch of his hand as he stroked my bare arm with his hot fingertips cut through my anger.

Shiver.

"I'm fine," I snapped. "Or I will be once these morons drop the damned honor crap and start getting their act together."

He nodded, blonde hair swinging over his shoulder, so close to me the silky strands brushed my skin. My demon hummed happily, distracted by his scent and the heat of his body.

How nice for her.

"Come," he said, taking my hand, threading his fingers through mine, smile still there, a deeper beckoning reflected in his pale eyes. "Let's see if we can start them down that road."

I should have pulled my hand free. Instead, I went with him, absorbing his warmth while my conscience tsked at me and reminded me I had a boyfriend already.

Didn't I?

chapter nineteen

We didn't return to the study, but retreated back toward the front of the house and through another doorway, into a wide foyer. I saw an open pair of doors on the far side, more light reaching us, and realized we'd only been in one wing of the big house. I pulled my hand free of Piers's as we entered what looked like a dining room. But there was no food on the table, much to my stomach's displeasure. Instead, a large map of the countryside spread over its surface, the palace in the center.

It was even bigger than I thought, if I was reading the scale of the map correctly. Had to be larger than a couple of football fields. Who lived in such opulence?

As much as I loved Charlotte and everything, part of me had to agree with the revolution, which brought down the Romanovs, if this was their idea of a country house.

A short, narrow-shouldered sorcerer, his red hair and freckles making him seem younger than he probably was squinted at Piers through his round glasses, a glare of light reflecting from the smooth twin surfaces.

"Sydlynn Hayle," Piers said, gesturing to his friend. "Allow me to introduce you to my team. This is Ellis Lowsley." Ginger nodded, hands spread out on the table before him. "Flora Husher." The pretty brunette's dark bob reminded me of an old friend and, in a rush of emotion, I missed Beth and wondered how she was.

"And this is Liard Meath." Crooked teeth grinned at me, his dark skin and brown eyes betraying his Indian heritage. Which made me think of Shenka,

Seriously, Syd? Find some freaking focus already.

"Last but not least, Perty Lins." Blonde, pert, pretty. I smiled a little and nodded to each of them, certain I'd forget their names in about two seconds even as I wondered why they all seemed so young. Where were the older Steam Union members?

Piers leaned over the table as Oleksander chewed the rim of his mustache, scowling at the map.

"Els," Piers said to the red-haired sorcerer. "Lay it out for us, if you would."

Ellis nodded, straightened up. "Our previous plan had to be altered, thanks to our new information." He gestured at me. Isabelle huddled next to him, misery on her face as she stared at the map herself. "Our main target remains the same, but we need to be more careful if the Czar is able to call on backup."

"Where are they holding Charlotte?" I peered at the map in frustration.

"We're not sure." Ellis might not have been, but Isabelle twitched with guilt and refused to meet my eyes. "But we'll find her once our main target is taken out."

Hang on. "Wait a second," I said, crossing my arms over my chest as I glared at Ellis. "Charlotte is the main target."

Piers hesitated before leaning close to me. "Actually," he said. "That's not exactly accurate."

What the hell?

"Our goal has always been to remove the Czar," Oleksander said, looking back and forth between Piers and me, confusion mingling with worry on his face. "Yes, my granddaughter is a priority, of course. But she would be the first to tell you the only way to free her would be to kill her oppressor."

Oh *hell* no.

Killing was not on the menu.

I didn't say a word, just spun on my heel and marched out. I felt someone following me, was grasped and turned around before I could make it half way across the foyer. I spun on Piers with a snarl on my lips as he pulled me to a halt.

"Please," he said, voice low and urgent, "allow me to

I jerked my arm free of his grip and hissed up into his handsome face. "Explain?" My whisper was so loud I knew the others heard me in the dining room, but I could barely contain my fury even as Oleksander came to stand in the doorway, watching, listening with a scowl on his face. "What's to explain, Piers?" I shook with anger, wanting to wring his damned neck. What was he thinking? "You kidnapped my ass, promising it was because you wanted to help me rescue Charlotte."

"I do," he said. "We will. It's just—"

"Just." I jabbed him in the chest with one stiff finger. "Just nothing, smartass. You do realize you're asking me, a foreign power, to interfere with another magical race." Was he off his rocker? "You want me," I poked him again, a little Sidhe power behind it, saw him wince, "to break all kinds of international magic laws so you," this jab had to hurt, the thud of impact making my own finger ache, "can take down a sect your people should have dealt with in the first place."

The air beside us shuddered as Isabelle appeared. She grasped my arm, pulled me away from Piers. "She can't get involved this way," the vampire said. "You know that. I told you already she would turn you down if she knew the truth."

Piers's jaw jumped as anger snapped in his gray eyes. But, to his credit, he took hold of his temper and blew out a whistling breath between tight lips before speaking.

"We'll fail without you." He backed off a step, shoulders tense while the guttural sound of Oleksander's startled grunt echoed softly to me. I guess Piers hadn't been forthcoming with any of us on this little adventure he'd concocted. "It's that simple."

"I'm sorry." I turned away from him, glanced back at the towering werewolf leader. "I'm only here for Charlotte."

"I'd heard you were the one to do the impossible." Oh no, he did *not*. "The one who took on the rules and won. Who did what was right," he almost spit the word, "not what was law."

I spun back, shaking with rage, hating he poked at my weakest points like any of this was my fault. "Don't you think I want to grind Yure under my heel until he's a smear for what he's done to Charlotte?" Piers's face remained flat, stony as I went on. "I'm not a total moron. I know the guy is a dirtbag who deserves what he gets. And were he in my territory, he'd be toast. End of story." I backed off again, frustrated, irritable. "But we're not on my turf, are we? And unless you want a war between territories, you're on your own."

Piers swayed, face crumpling as he reached for me. I let him take my hands, felt his need, the power of his conviction, his own determination. He reminded me a lot of me, actually. Standing against wrongs that needed righting no matter the odds against him. It broke my heart to have to turn him down.

"We'll hide you," he said, his desperation coming through. "With our power. And as long as you don't use witch magic, there's no harm, no foul." So he knew about that, huh? Isabelle flinched, guilty. Was there anything she hadn't told him?

I thought about it. I really, honestly did. But, in the end, my mind went to my mother, to our own battles, the fight yet to come with the Brotherhood and Ameline, and I knew I had no choice either.

His warm hands fell from mine as I pulled away for the last time. "I'm sorry, Piers," I said. "I really am. But this isn't my fight." I turned to Isabelle. "I'm going after Charlotte," I said. "And I need your help to find her."

The young vampire ducked her head, but nodded.

I left him there, heard his footsteps as he turned and walked away himself, kept a firm grip on Isabelle as we left the foyer and reentered the hall near the red door.

"Okay," I said, trying to push down the horrible guilt in the core of my stomach at the thought of not being able to help the werewolves. Wasn't Piers right? I was the one who said screw the rules and did what I wanted anyway. When did I become the person who had to say no when there was work to be done? Not fair, nope. I'd saved the world and my family more times than I cared to count, kicked more bad guy butt than anyone in this house. And yet...

What had I told Vasyl? I didn't do 'no'.

Guess I was wrong.

I gave myself a little shake as I fixed the young vampire with my sternest Mom glare.

"I know you know where she is, Isabelle." Time to beat myself up later. At least with Charlotte to focus on, I could forget for a bit the hurt and desperate look on Piers's handsome face. "I need you to tell me."

Isabelle trembled. "I don't know if I can trust what Maksym told me any longer." She shuddered before taking my hand. "But I can get you past the guards into the black zone."

"Black zone?" I reached for the veil, felt it answer my call, but didn't open it yet. I had an idea I wanted to try, but I needed a target first before I could test it.

"The place where no magic can see," Isabelle said.

Must be shielded with sorcery. Probably like the Coterie Industries building in Miami and the now burned down Brotherhood mansion. I could handle any dead area cut off from regular magicks, as long as I knew where it was. Too risky sniffing around on my own, but with guidance, I could pinpoint the location and attempt a focused peek at Charlotte's situation.

At least, that was the hope.

Isabelle showed me, her vampire magic linking with mine. Piggybacking on her power felt weird, but wasn't the strangest thing I'd ever done so I just held on and kept my senses open. It wasn't long before her power flowed onto the Czar's property and to the palace. I shuddered as we rounded the far side and hit a cold, black zone.

My turn. I filtered my sorcery through Isabelle's vampire magic, hoping to disguise it, and had a peek. Shivered as the darkness parted and I had my first look at the cellblock. The feeling of emptiness confirmed my guess about the shielding. Isabelle chased back to our location, a straight line to where I could find Charlotte before releasing me.

I hugged her on impulse, felt her strong, thin arms embrace me in turn.

"Thank you," I said, leaning away. "I need one more favor."

She nodded quickly.

"Go home," I said. "Tell Sunny what's happening. And stay there."

Isabelle's eyes welled with tears. "I can't leave Maksym."

Whatever. "Let the Steam Union do their jobs," I said. "Just go home, Isabelle."

She let out a soft sob before shuddering into shadow and vanishing.

I did my best to protect her. What she did was up to her.

Time to finally rescue Charlotte and get the hell out of here before something else happened.

CHAPTER TWENTY

I walked back down the hall to the bedroom I'd found, grateful Raoul was long gone. The door snicked shut behind me as I used a little magic to lock it.

Reasonably sure now I wouldn't be disturbed, I reached for the veil and tore it open. Ahbi's power poured out toward me, my demon grandmother's spirit now part of the Node keeping Demonicon's multiple planes stable. I held back as she tried to draw me into the veil, instead allowing my demon ego to connect with her.

"Grandmother." I felt her power ripple, pause, listen. "I need a favor."

Her magic shuddered, hugged me.

"My friend Charlotte has been kidnapped." I let Ahbi feel Charlotte as a reminder, but she shoved that aside with impatience. Okay then, she got the message, knew exactly who I was talking about. The flashing image of my werefriend as a freaky creature with black scales and oddly jointed legs made me shudder. "Right," I said. "Exactly."

Her magic prodded me, now impatient. Nice to know some things never changed. Ahbi Sanghamitra had been powerful and commanding in life and was no different now only her spirit survived. Though I kind of loved her this way, to my delight.

Weird to prefer my demon grandmother dead to alive?

Tell me about it.

"I need to see where she is before I go to her so I know if it's safe to rescue her."

Ahbi's magic seemed to mull that over. I traced the path Isabelle showed me, sharing it with her, all the way to the black zone. Ahbi's magic balked, angry.

"I know," I said, feeling a little self-conscious about talking to her out loud, not sure why I didn't just speak mentally like I did with others. As odd as it was, it somehow felt comforting to use my physical voice with her. "But I have sorcery, remember?" I opened the blossom of darkness beneath me. She felt it, shivered back from it. "I think I can link you to it, enough you can see through for me. But you can't tear the veil all the way on the other side. Just enough for a glimpse."

Siphon. Her voice whispered in my head.

Right. "I think I can keep it from taking any of your

power," I said. "I know it means risking the Node's balance, but it could also mean the difference between war and peace on my end." I needed to get in and out fast, without being spotted, if this was to work. Of course, Applegate would know I was the one who rescued Charlotte, but she'd have no proof and neither would the Czar if I could nab the weregirl without being spotted.

At least, if this worked.

Ahbi's magic surged around me again. *Try.*

Awesome. The only real stumbling block to the plan had been Ahbi's agreement. Now I had it, I could see if my theory was correct.

I'd been riding the veil for years, going to and fro without really thinking about how it worked. When I'd gone after the Brotherhood the first time, I'd been able to use Demetrius's guidance to tell the veil where I wanted to go. But I'd always wondered if there were other uses.

Including spying. I hadn't had the opportunity or reason, until now, to give it a try. But as far as I could tell, my idea was sound. The veil opened on my end, carried me to my destination as it sealed behind me, then tore on the other end and let me out. So why couldn't I open two tears at once and have a look between them?

I was about to find out. From the curiosity in Ahbi's power, she hadn't thought of using the veil this way before either. Made me chuckle to myself. Had she, I was sure she'd have used it to her absolute advantage while she'd still been alive and Ruler of Demonicon.

Carefully, with my vampire, demon and Shaylee all forming a protective shield between my grandmother and my sorcery, I opened the tiniest sliver and linked her to my dark magic. For a moment, she shuddered, the tear in the veil wavering even as my sorcery surged, starving for what Ahbi and the Node had to offer. But the pressure of my other magicks held it back just enough Ahbi was able to latch on and complete the link.

I eased back, my egos, too, until the shielding was gone. Weird, having Ahbi's power pulse inside mine. I'd carried her soul for a while, back when she was first murdered by Ameline, but this was far different. She was connected to all the magic on Demonicon through the Node. And now, she had sorcery at her disposal.

I grinned at the thought of my grandmother's spirit now having access to the one power we all feared and hoped her brilliant mind, obviously still awake and aware, could somehow come up with the means to use that knowledge to our advantage.

Ahbi wasted no time, the glow of amber fire of the tear flashing with images. I held my breath, stomach clenched. This idea of mine was a long shot, but it looked like it just might work.

I gasped a deep breath of air as the flickering view solidified, firmed up.

And Charlotte appeared. The image was dull, dark, a narrow tunnel. Ahbi had to be keeping the tear on the other side to a minimum as requested, but I didn't expect it would take long for someone to notice, so we had to hurry.

A quick hug for Ahbi was returned as I forced myself to slow down, catch my breath as my heart pounded in relief.

"Can we have a look around her?" Ahbi was one step ahead of me, already panning the view even as I spoke. My werefriend sat in a cell, bars making her door, though she had a canopied bed and a tall, narrow window shrouded in a curtain, as though the Czar made some attempt to give her small comforts despite her captivity.

Sick bastard.

Charlotte was alone, eyes downcast. She didn't look up or take notice I was watching. Maybe for the best.

"Okay, Ahbi," I said. "Let me through."

I leaped into the veil, followed the set path and, within a heartbeat, stepped out of the tear on the other side and into Charlotte's cell.

She looked up, eyes huge as I quickly glanced around, the hole still open, waiting for our retreat. I grinned at my friend, holding out my hand to her even as I kept one foot inside the veil.

"Hey, Charlotte," I said. "Nice to see you. Coming?"

I watched the shock in her eyes turn to despair as she

turned her head away.

"I can't," she whispered.

Holy. Freaking. Elements.

"Raoul is fine," I said, glancing out through the bars. Any second now someone could show up. We didn't have time to discuss this. "So you don't have to stay."

Charlotte didn't react, hugging herself, huddling into a small, compact heap.

"I know," she said, voice breaking.

My anger crackled around me, sparks falling to the stone floor as my frustration got the better of me. "Okay then," I said. "Get your ass over here and let's go."

A headshake. Was she kidding me here?

Damn it, I knew this might be a fight. But I didn't expect Charlotte to be an idiot.

"The bond is broken," she said, tears in her voice. "I failed you. I deserve what I get."

Choke. Splutter.

"I watched it happen," she went on, a thin wail rising through her words. "I felt you drift from me, further and further. Leaving me behind." She turned back, face a mask of grief, tears streaming down her face, so young looking, frail, beaten. "You don't need me and I failed you." Charlotte's hands shook as she held them out to me. "You were shot." She shuddered. "Shot. And I was too late, Syd, too late to protect you." Her accent thickened with her voice as she struggled to swallow.

"This is all my fault, you almost died, my mother did, Danilo." She sobbed, a wrenching sound as though her insides were torn in half. "I failed all of you and I deserve what I get!"

I gaped at her, anger falling away. I'd never seen her so emotional. Hell, I rarely saw her crack a smile, as far as that went. Her wolf emerged, whining like a beaten puppy, only to retreat again as she clawed at the metal collar around her neck.

I didn't have time for her pity party. As hard as it was, I shoved aside my own emotions and reached out to her with my spirit magic, feeling along the edges of the collar.

It's keeping her from shifting, my vampire sent, sympathy aching inside me.

I think it's making her a dumbass, my demon snarled. *Cut that thing loose and let's hit the road already.*

"Charlotte." I left the edge of the veil, felt Ahbi reaching for me, anxious, trying to pull me back. "We have to go." Sigh. "We've been through so much. Don't quit on me now."

Her shoulders twitched, though her broken expression didn't change.

"Don't quit on your people." If I had to flog her with guilt to get her to act, I would.

Another twitch. She turned her head away. "They are better off without me."

"They beg to differ." What would it take? This wasn't

my Charlotte. Maybe my demon was right. Maybe the collar was affecting her. After all, the Brotherhood were known for their subtle manipulations, weren't they? But when I let my vampire's magic try to sever the metal, Charlotte cried out and grasped at the collar again.

There has to be another way, my vampire sent. *Your sorcery perhaps?*

It will have to wait. Shaylee's concern cut through my emotions like a cold splash of water. Vibrations beneath us. *Someone is coming.*

Out of time.

"I'm not strong enough to lead them." Charlotte's self-flagellation was getting a little old, frankly. "I know that now."

"What the hell happened to the weregirl who didn't take crap from anyone?" I could feel the approaching feet now, thankful for Shaylee's early warning system. "They're coming for you, the family you seem to have written off, so you'd better be damned ready to fight."

Charlotte's head whipped around, desperate fear on her face. "No," she whispered. "They can't."

"Well, they are." I crossed my arms over my chest, forcing myself to calm despite the approaching feet. Which slowed. Stopped. Okay then. Luck was on our side. No clue how much time we had, but Charlotte better smarten the hell up or I was knocking her over the head and dragging her out of there.

Charlotte leaped to her feet and grabbed my arms in her hands, shaking me. "They can't," she sobbed. "Yure knows they are coming. He's ready for them."

Piers was in for more than he bargained for, then. I forced aside my need to warn him. I had to focus on Charlotte. But she clung to me, still shaking me, fingers digging into my bare flesh.

"Please." She fell to her knees at my feet. "Please, you have to stop them. He will kill them all."

"Charlotte," I said. "They aren't my problem." I reached for her as gently as I could. "You are."

She surged to her feet, face twisting in anger. Charlotte lunged for the bars, screaming at the top of her lungs in Ukrainian. I felt the shiver of the ground as the feet that approached doubled, tripled in number.

Out of time.

She spun on me, frantic. "Save them," she said.

Damn her. A flicker of motion around the far corner and I was sunk. Kicking myself for not just grabbing her when I had the chance, I ducked back into the veil and ran for the werewolves to warn them.

This was just not my night.

chapter twenty one

The moment I landed back in the bedroom, I knew I was too late. The touch of werewolf and sorcery was gone. I jerked the door open after swearing at the lock I myself engaged, racing down the hall and into the foyer, reaching for Piers even though I knew he was gone.

They all were. Didn't take them long to clear out, either. I stood in the empty dining room, maps still spread out, and knew I'd pushed the young sorcerer to act impetuously by denying his request for help.

Damn it, he was going to get them all killed.

I spun, reaching for the veil, ready to chase them down and stop them.

Only to slam into a flare of blue magic that sent me flying backward. Stars burst in my vision as I impacted the doorjamb, body going limp. I sagged to the floor, spine on fire as Finlay and Gwendolyn appeared in the foyer in that same flare of magic.

The young witch ran to my side, falling to her knees beside me as I fought to stay conscious. My head rang, the clunk to my skull enough to shake my focus. My vampire did her best to fix the damage quickly, but I was already being lifted into Finlay's arms, his power wrapping around me before she could complete the healing.

Flaring once again.

I tried to fight him off as the big Enforcer set me on the bed. The inn again, the same suite I'd been kidnapped from. Was it really only a few hours ago? My vampire cursed softly as she finally healed me, my awareness coming into sharp focus.

"Let me go." I shoved Finlay aside, almost ran into Gwendolyn who reached for me, worry creasing her face.

"Are you all right?" Her voice shook as she spoke. It wasn't until I looked up and around I realized we weren't alone. The room was full of witches, both local and Enforcer. Nataliya wrung her hands over and over, tears standing in her eyes while Fedir patted her shoulder in an endless attempt at comfort. "We've been searching everywhere for you."

Could this night really get any worse? "I have to go." I tried to shove past Gwendolyn, felt a bubble of Enforcer magic flare to life around the room.

"You're not going anywhere." Finlay's gruff voice made me snarl.

"Like hell." I jerked free of his grip as he reached for me. "Back off."

"Sydlynn." Gwendolyn's worry turned to hurt. "We came to save you."

"Thanks for that." Okay, it wasn't her fault, not really. But Charlotte was still captive and, if my werefriend was right, Piers and her family were walking into a trap. I had to go, damn it.

I reached for Piers again, only to run right into the same bubble of witch power.

"For your own protection," Gwendolyn said. I'm sure she meant to be soothing, the way she patted my hand. Like I was some frightened kitten needing to be coaxed into trust with a soothing pet.

"Listen to me." I reached out and grabbed her like she'd grabbed me, ignoring Finlay's growl of warning. "You have no idea what's going on out there." The bubble taunted me. I could break through it easily, of course I could. But doing so meant taking that final step. Expulsion from Europe and war.

"We know the Czar has been difficult." Gwendolyn gently detached herself from my grip as the gathered witches and Enforcers stared at me like I'd lost my mind.

Was about to, thanks.

She had no clue, none of them did. That the Czar was owned by the Brotherhood. Would it be worth it to tell them? I met Gwendolyn's eyes, Finlay's. The other gathered witches and Enforcers who looked alarmed, but not for me.

Because of me.

They wouldn't listen. No more than the two who were charged with tying my hands behind my back listened when I'd berated them only a few hours earlier in this very room. I scowled at the missing furniture wreckage, evidence of my loss of temper wiped clean, replaced with a new chair.

As if nothing happened. As though none of what was going on beyond these walls mattered.

Sometimes I really hated my kind for their shortsighted lack of willingness to care about anyone but their own damned outdated laws. Had finally dealt with this same mess at home only to have to face it all over again.

Déjà vu I could do without.

I could have told them about the Czar, the Brotherhood connection, my suspicions this wasn't about Charlotte at all, but about me and the final battle to come. But I just didn't have the energy to expend on wasted breath and effort.

Hope died. I'd fought so hard for so long, only to be right back where I'd started. Yet again, things had gone so far out to left field I was sure now they would never come back. But.

But.

Head shake. This wasn't my fight. I had a larger picture to observe, didn't I? The werewolves, the Steam Union. None of them were part of what I had to do, at least, not according to Iepa. They might have to fight if I failed, but I wasn't planning on failing. I really should just stand down, focus on what I had to be prepared for, my job ahead. The last battle with the Brotherhood. With Ameline and the two sides of the maji.

The grand scheme called me. Mocked me. Rubbed me the wrong way for the last time.

To hell with it.

Something fluttered in the air, shadow trying to take form. I caught the briefest touch from Isabelle as I reached for her with my vampire power, slicing the tiniest hole in the edge of the bubble.

Please.

It was the only word to make it through. That and the snapshot of the scene at the front of the palace. Falling werewolves dying under gunfire, pops of light cutting the night. The surging black of sorcery devouring everything.

Piers. Oleksander.

Aw, crap.

I reached for the veil, felt Finlay's magic try to stop me. Brushed aside the surge of rage Applegate aimed at me as I reached for Ahbi and jerked open a hole in the bubble. Dove into the welcoming amber fire to the sound of Gwendolyn calling my name and was gone.

chapter twenty two

Ahbi dumped me out of the veil just inside the tree line, within sight of the front entry to the palace, but out of the fight. I let out a shriek from the sudden cold, forgetting, in my dash for freedom, I'd lost my jacket back at the farmhouse. Ahbi snarled, her power surging around me. A film of heat pushed back the icy winter night and cocooned me in warmth. I hugged her and let her go, feeling her anxiety for me, but knowing I had to act.

Damn Piers Southway for needing me to rescue him.

I locked onto his sorcery, only beginning to be able to differentiate between gaping holes of nothing. His had the same subtle taste of mint around the edges. I brushed two others, could only guess they were his friends and not his enemies, and threw up all the shielding I could before making a dash for his position.

Bullets ricocheted from my wards, bouncing free in showers of sparks. It was my sorcery's idea to absorb the energy from the bullets, pumping up the power it had available with every strike. Not that being shot at was ever a good thing, but at least I gained some benefit from it.

I felt like an idiot, zigzagging my way across the snow toward two SUV's parked at angles to each other. Both rocked over and over with the impact of black balls of sorcery, and I knew the metal could only hold out for so long before it collapsed, the energy inside it spent. Cold bit through the edges of Ahbi's magic, even reinforced by my demon.

The cocoon wouldn't last long. I had to get shelter or find a new coat before I froze to death.

The sight of a trio of werewolves creeping up behind Piers made me lunge forward even faster, my demon pushing against me to give me extra speed. My last mad dash drew fire as I rushed past the weres, buffeting them with spirit magic on the way by. I slid forward, slamming into Piers from behind. He cried out as I grasped his jacket in both hands, covering him with my shielding as we both spun and attacked the rapidly recovering, gun-wielding werewolves together. My peripheral mind wondered why they didn't just morph into wolf form and take us out instead of trusting to the artillery they carried. Werewolves didn't need guns. But I didn't have time to thrash it out. The sneaky threesome cried out as Piers shattered their weapons with his power while another blast of Sidhe energy embedded their writhing bodies in steaming ground. I melted the remains of their weapons to slag with demon fire while they sagged, unconscious, Piers's sorcery draining them of energy.

"About time you showed up." His harsh words were paired with a tight grin.

"Are you a total moron or just an idiot in training?" I slashed at the ball of sorcery heading for us, cutting it off before it could hit the SUV we crouched behind. The vehicle rocked anyway, tires blowing on the other side. A good thing, as the chassis sank to the snow, cutting off the path of magic under the bulk of the truck.

"What?" He tensed as the truck rocked again, focusing on the power flowing through the metal and into his hands, absorbing it before lobbing his own over the roof in a random attack. "You've never seen a knight in shining armor before?"

I rolled my eyes, jerking him back from peeking around the back corner of the truck as a hail of bullets met him. "Don't be a jerk," I said. Looked around with growing concern. "Where are the werewolves?"

Piers's shoulders twitched. "Captured," he said. "I tried to talk Oleksander and the others into staying behind, wanted to try a sneak attack, but he insisted." He blew a breath through pursed lips, soft whistle escaping.

"The Czar was ready for us."

Reality hit finally, did it?

"I tried to warn you," I said. "But I was captured by the Enforcers. Took me a bit to escape."

"As soon as we arrived, Yure appeared and ordered Oleksander and Raoul to heel." Piers shivered, rage in his face. "Like they were dogs."

Unfortunately, that was all they were to the Czar.

"That left the four of us to do our best," Piers said as the truck rocked, hitting him hard in the shoulder. "I know we should have just run, but..." Yeah. I totally understood.

A glance right and left turned up his three sorcerer friends, the young red-head passed out in the lap of the girl with the bob. Damn it, what was her name?

"What about the rest of your people?" Surely the Steam Union was way more than five young adults with delusions of white knighthood.

Piers winced, and not just from the blow to the truck that shoved it back two feet, forcing us to scramble with it.

"Ah," he said. "About that."

I had a feeling I was not going to like what he said next.

"As it happens," he went on, "we're not exactly here with permission."

Oh. My. Swearword.

"You didn't." Go away, surge of respect and kinship. No time for you right now.

He shrugged, braced himself and lobbed off another ball of black. "I tried to convince her," he said. "Did my best. When Danilo came to us, I almost had her. But she caved when he was killed." Piers's gray eyes, almost silver in the moonlight reflected from the snow, caught and held mine. "I just couldn't let it stand, Syd."

Sounds familiar, my vampire sent.

Vaguely. My demon's chuckle was wicked.

Oh dear, Shaylee sent. Sighed. *Another one. Will we survive?*

Smartasses.

"Who's 'she'?" My shields repelled one more volley of bullets as I snapped off some demon fire at a pair of werewolves trying to circle around like the unlucky three buried to their armpits in steaming earth. They flew back, crashing into a fountain, the statue toppling over on top of them with a resounding crash.

Piers sighed. "My mum," he said. "Eva Southway. The leader of our branch of the Union."

I snorted. Couldn't help myself. Burst into laughter at the absolute irony of it all. Piers stared at me a moment as though I'd cracked before laughing himself.

"You'll have to tell me why that was so funny," he said, eyes sparkling. "Sometime."

"Not now." I kept grinning.

"There are Steam Union in your part of the world trying to fight back." He motioned for his friends to back off. Ellis had woken, nodded groggily as the four sank into black and vanished. "But my people won't help." He turned to me. "It's just you and me now, Sydlynn Hayle. I won't put them at risk any more. I'll take all the responsibility for what's happening. But I can't walk away."

My demon hummed happily, giving me a shove toward the inevitable. She didn't need to. I was already kissing him.

Syd. Battle. Remember? Dying, fighting, bullets...

Piers's lips were hot, so hot, burning through the edge of the cocoon Ahbi created around me. As hot as other lips I knew and loved. Like we had time for this. But I just couldn't help myself, not when he was so in tune with my mind I wondered where he'd been all my life.

I jerked away as the SUV spun sideways, pulling Piers along with me as I tore open the veil and dove through. He didn't fight me, to his credit, though I felt him shiver beside me as I dumped us out again.

Into more snow. Back where I started at the edge of the trees, the front of the palace bathed in the crackle of fire as one of the SUV's exploded, the body bursting outward in a hail of giant shrapnel. Piers stared at the mess he'd made for a long moment before sagging to a crouch, head down, elbows on his knees.

"I failed Danilo," he said.

Considering he had a handful of young sorcerers and a pack of weres the Czar could control as his only backup, he was being pretty hard on himself. The worst part was how familiar he sounded. Heard that before, just recently. Wasn't taking it from him, either.

"Cut yourself some slack," I said. "You're alive, aren't you?"

"I promised Danilo," Piers said, turning to meet my eyes, his glistening with frustration and extra moisture. "I did my best to convince Mum, but she refused. I couldn't just let his people suffer this way, Syd." His hands clenched at his sides. "I should have known better. I'm an idiot."

He could say that again.

"You want to make a dent in this disaster or not?" I prodded him with one foot. He glanced up at me, shrugged with a slow smile. Stood to his full height, now looking down on me. The moonlight on his face really made him rather beautiful—

I snapped at my demon who sighed and shrugged. She had the worst freaking timing.

I took his hand this time, letting him lace his fingers through mine, welcoming the heat of his skin as the cocoon began to crumble.

"Hang on," I said. "And be ready for anything."

How much did I love he just grinned and followed?

chapter twenty three

I tore open the veil and addressed my grandmother. "Okay, Ahbi," I said. "Where can you put us inside the palace that won't land us in the middle of a battle?"

She hummed and hawed a moment and, I swear, was actually enjoying herself. Piers's frown told me he was more than a little confused, but he held his silence, bless him.

When the flickering image settled, we were looking at what seemed to be a kitchen. Empty. At least, for now.

"Perfect." I pulled Piers through the veil before he could think to speak up after all and stepped out again on the other side into the quiet room. The veil sealed shut behind us, Ahbi's power ghosting over Piers and me before she hugged me and was gone.

"That was..." Piers's whisper tickled my ear as he bent to speak.

"My grandmother," I whispered back. "Yeah, she's dead. Don't ask." I shrugged. "Let's go."

The door at the far end of the dark kitchen opened into an equally dark hallway.

"Any idea where we are?" Piers looked left and right. The elaborate décor of the main part of the palace was missing here, so I took a guess.

"Somewhere away from Yure's main stomping grounds." I let the kitchen door swing softly shut behind me. Did my best to perform a light exam of our surroundings. Difficult considering how heavy-handed I usually was with my magic. I brushed the familiar touch of the black zone as my hopes rose rapidly despite my attempt to hold any expectation of success behind a wall of tough girl Syd. "But close to Charlotte."

Piers followed my lead, his sorcery held in a tight net around him. I released the last of Ahbi's cocoon, no longer needing it, though the air in this part of the palace felt chilly, giving me the impression this wing didn't see much use.

"You know," Piers said, amusement in his voice despite our situation, "we seem to make an excellent team."

I snorted. "You mean, you do a good job of getting into trouble and I do a good job rescuing you."

His magic prodded me. "If you like. But I think you're underestimating me, Coven Leader."

We'd just see about that.

I felt the push of sorcery coming toward me, too late. Two skinny men flanked by a pair of hulking weres with guns burst around the corner ahead of us. The lead one pointed, shouted in Ukrainian while the guns blazed. My shields held while Piers dove to the ground, his magic seeping across the floor and under their feet. Shock rippled over the four faces as the floor beneath them almost immediately gave way, Shaylee adding a little extra zing to Piers's attack. Machine gun fire rattled into the ceiling as they disappeared through a large sinkhole and out of sight.

Kind of comical, actually. Like watching a cartoon.

Piers sprang to his feet and ran lightly forward, his long coat belling out behind him like a cloak. I followed, accepting his hand as he leaped across the gap, pulling me over with him. One look down and my vertigo kicked in, flickers of falling the endless drop from the top of the Seat on Demonicon to the Parade below. Made worse by the sight of the four bodies sprawled in what looked like some kind of dimly lit cellar.

Nothing funny about their twisted bodies after all, the scent of blood rising to tingle my sensitive vampire nose.

I wavered on the other side of the hole Piers had made, stomach rolling, caught in the flashback of my plummet to near death. Piers grasped me around the waist and tucked me against him, lips against my ear before he leaned back. His nose brushed mine, we were so close, his smile wicked as I panted into his mouth.

"You were saying about doing the rescuing?" Piers let me go, but took my hand again as the last tingle of my fear vanished at his touch. The linking of our fingers felt way too natural for a girl with a boyfriend who wasn't the one holding her hand.

I tried to pull Piers toward the black zone when we reached the end of the hall, but he fought me, shaking his head.

"None of this will matter if the Czar escapes." His handsome face pleaded with me, free hand rising to stroke my cheek. "His people will back off if he falls." Another stroke. "Please."

Sigh.

It was absolutely the wrong decision to make and pretty much guaranteed to start a war, but I agreed with his choice, damn it.

Charlotte would have to wait.

The fact I'd just committed myself to a fight I really should have run from screaming wasn't lost on me. Especially when someone cut through my shields in a surge of familiar power and blasted me one as a reminder.

What the hell do you think you're doing? Mom's anger was so powerful I flinched and pulled free of Piers in a reflex guilt action. He stopped, turned to frown at me, froze as I made a "we're screwed" face and tucked up against a wall to take my punishment. *I said quietly. Didn't I say quietly, Syd?*

Hey, Mom. Yeah, like the whole innocent routine was going to do me any good. *I didn't have much choice.*

Mom's sigh echoed across the distance. *Why is it you never seem to have any other option than total mayhem?* Her laughter came out breathless. *Well, whatever it is you have planned, you'd better hurry up, my darling daughter. Margaret was just here, and she's screaming bloody murder.*

You let her go? I tsked, amazed how well she was taking this and how much humor rippled through the connection between us as her initial jolt of alarm wore off. *Mom, you're slipping.*

I have no idea why I was struggling to keep a straight face and attitude all of a sudden, but Mom giggled, near hysterical herself.

You should have seen her, she sent. *All red faced and foaming at the mouth. Spectacular.*

You're one to talk, I sent back with a snicker. *You're forgetting your own little meltdowns were a sight to behold.* It shouldn't have been funny. Mom almost lost herself to the Brotherhood completely.

And yet, here we were, laughing ourselves into tears of hilarity.

Hysterics. Had to be. But the laughter helped to shake off my nerves and charge up my focus.

Hers too, I guess. She cleared her mental throat after

a moment of snorting. *Syd, I'm serious.*

Me too. I gave Piers a push and got moving again. *Charlotte wouldn't leave, the young Steam Union idiot I'm saddled with bit off more than he could chew and the weres are now captured. You wanted me to leave them?*

I thought we agreed the werewolves weren't our problem. She sighed. Laughed again. *I should have known our agreement wouldn't last, not when there are innocent lives at stake.* She hugged me tight with her magic. *Sweetheart, you know I'm behind you, no matter what happens.* Mom's power finally released me. *Just be careful.*

Piers glanced back at me as I severed the connection.

"Let me guess," he said with a grin. "You have a mother just like mine."

He clearly knew that already. "Not quite," I said. "Mine just gave me the go-ahead to dismantle the world order and to hell with the consequences."

"Lucky," he said.

"Am I ever." My grin was tight with renewed tension and the need to act. "But we're about to have company who thinks to the contrary, so we'd better hurry."

I hated not having access to my full magic, fought with the idea of breaking the last mandate Applegate set and just say screw it. But as long as I kept my witch magic—read maji power—under wraps while I was here, the worst she could do was boot my ass from Europe forever. She'd have to catch me first.

CHAPTER TWENTY FOUR

I should have seen it coming and probably would have if Shaylee hadn't been keeping a vibrations ear open behind us in case of pursuit. Besides, I was a little busy working out how I was going to free Charlotte and the werewolves while helping Piers bring down the Czar without backup and no maji power.

It was a lot to juggle *and* pay attention to where we were headed and who we might run into. I was counting on Piers to handle at least one of those jobs. Otherwise, why did I drag him along again?

Oh, wait. He dragged me along.

Right.

My vampire's hiss was all the warning I had as we rounded the next corner into an atrium of some kind, filled with doorways leading elsewhere. Some kind of wing hub to the rest of the palace was my guess.

Well, my peripheral mind guessed. The rest of me snapped into focus on the dozen werewolves and two sorcerers hovering in the middle of the grand space.

Oops. Good thing my shields were so strong. My sorcery gobbled the kinetic energy from the immediate flow of bullets, though the wards could do little to give me my hearing back as the machine gun fire echoed from the marble floor and glass dome overhead. Piers's magic slid outward, and the pool of black grew into an attack that had become old already. I wondered if he was a one-trick pony.

The first sorcerer cracked a whip, slicing across the back of one of the werewolves. The were howled in pain, the sound so loud I heard it over the gunfire. He dropped his weapon, writhing, hands pressed to his face as his body jerked and heaved. His transformation into wolf shape tore the clothes from his body, sending him to a low crouch. Half-shifted, face a distorted mix of canine and human, the wereguard lunged at us, long, sharp claws outstretched.

Disgust made my stomach clench as my vampire formed a fist of white power and slammed it into the approaching werewolf, sending him back into his friends. Likely with a few bullets in his back and a crushed sternum. And no, my disgust wasn't aimed at the were, but at his handler.

So this is why they hadn't attacked us outside in wolf

form. They were being controlled, their natural ability quashed and manipulated by the sorcerers who wrangled them. Still, it made no sense to hold them back when their shifting could hand over an advantage.

Unless.

The Brotherhood was involved. Which meant it was Liander Belaisle pulling the strings. Could he be trying to undermine Yure's position in his sick and subtle way? Made sense. Especially considering the Brotherhood's previous desire to absorb the Black Souls.

And the werewolves.

Oh. My. Swearword.

Belaisle wanted the weres to himself.

Another crack of the whip jarred me out of my thoughts as two more of the bulky guards shifted shape. Their handler sent them into the line of fire, too, a smirk on his nasty face. This time my demon roared in return, her own whips of amber flame lacing through the air, weaving together in a burning pattern we'd learned while fighting on Demonicon.

I couldn't let the weres fall into Belaisle's hands. They thought Yure and his people were cruel. But neither would I let them hurt me or stop me from achieving my goals.

Which meant fighting back.

The weres didn't stand a chance. And though I knew we'd win in the end against this group, the noise we made had to be summoning reinforcements. I didn't really feel like taking on the entire werewolf nation, thanks.

Piers grunted next to me, shuddered, panting. "He's countering me."

The second sorcerer's own black pool pushed against Piers's magic.

"So try something else." I didn't have time to talk him through battle strategy, in case he hadn't noticed. Damn it, this would be so much easier if I could just use my maji power. A few tweaks to my shields and a push of creation energy and this would be over.

No such luck.

One of the doors opened and three more werewolves burst through. Great, the cavalry started to arrive. But before I could focus some of my already divided attention on them, the one in the lead opened fire.

Not on us. On the two sorcerer handlers. The one with the whip spun on his attacker, snarling, lashing out with his sorcery. All three of the new weres fell to their knees, guns rattling to the ground, clutching their heads.

I had no idea if they were on our side or not, but I wasn't about to look a gift were in the mouth. My sorcery blocked the handler, slicing in between his magic and the three werewolves, slamming him back away from them. The sorcerer staggered, falling back into his partner, snapping the other man's attention.

Piers's grunt of success came the same moment the

first attacking werewolf shook his head, staggering to his feet, gun retrieved and raised. Before I could stop him, the hulking shifter rattled off a stream of bullets. I could only guess the sorcerer's shields were weakened from the fight with Piers and I, made worse by my companion's power now rippling under them and drawing on their magic. The two fell with screams of pain, blood bursting from the bullet shots that ripped through their wards, sending them to crash to the shattered marble tiles.

I watched, wincing in sympathy despite the circumstances, as the gathered werewolves turned and stared down at their former masters. Our rescuer strode across the floor, feet ringing on the stone in the sudden silence, standing over the two, gun muzzle inches from their faces.

"At last," he said. And pulled the trigger.

Gross. Just. Gross. I knew they had every right to want to kill the sorcerers who held them in thrall for so long, but it didn't mean I had to like the sight of blood and bits of brain matter splattered all over the floor.

Piers turned toward me, body curving around mine. Probably to protect me. Sigh. When would the guys in my life understand I didn't need protecting?

I pushed him away and approached the now silent werewolves, doing my best not to look down, though I slipped once on something I hoped wasn't part of someone.

Did I say gross?

Before I could speak a word, our rescuer bowed to me. "I am Maksym Rusak," he said. "My Isa told me you were our only hope."

I looked up into his burning green eyes and wavy brown hair, wide jaw and broad shoulders and understood Isabelle's attraction, at least. Not to mention the fact werewolves had a certain animal magnetism—

Syd. *Syd.* Sheesh.

"Thanks for the timely intervention." I sidestepped the edge of one of the sorcerer's robes to shake Maksym's hand.

He didn't release me, gripping my fingers tight, hope in his face. "She said you could free us."

Mutters from the others, the steady presence of Piers behind me as Shaylee spoke up.

I think it's time we talked to Galleytrot, she sent.

Now? She had to be out of it.

If we can free them completely, she sent, *that's a few more allies and a few less enemies. And I have a feeling we'll be needing some help in the next little while.*

Agreed, my vampire sent.

Need I remind you lot we're in the middle of a danger zone and, the amount of noise our little playmates here just made, I gestured at the werewolves who looked around at each other like I was crazy, *we're not likely to be alone much longer. Not to mention the fact Applegate could crash this little party any second now.*

All the more reason to stop gabbing and get to it. My demon's growl was tinged with amusement. *Why do you always argue with us when you know we'll get our way?*

Argh.

Fine. I jabbed Shaylee. *Prod the big dog and see what's up.*

It meant opening my shields again, but the girls thought it was worth it and, from the expectant frown on Maksym's face, this had better work or the allies we thought we'd gained could turn on us at any second.

Syd. Galleytrot's rumbling voice reached me, the faint scent of spring and fresh rain carried with him. *Are you all right?*

Not exactly, I sent. *Shocker, right?*

His deep chuckle answered like the sound of thunder.

But that can wait. I need your help. About thirty seconds of explaining later and he had the gist.

Yes, he sent. *I sensed there was more to the bond I severed than just to the Dumonts. But I didn't have time at that point to explore further.*

Think you can work your black hound magic with these guys? I tried a little smile and nod for Maksym as he stared at me, his friends growing more restless. "Just give me a second," I said out loud.

Let me feel them. The sound of sniffing accompanied my exploration, through Sidhe earth magic, of the bond inside the werewolves. It was as faint as the one I'd shared with Charlotte, hard to find. But beneath it, darkness eddied, the sorcery that created them holding them captive.

I can handle the bond that keeps them tied to individuals, Galleytrot sent. *But you will have to sever the one to their sorcerer creators.*

I'll follow your lead. I felt him swell inside me, linked with Shaylee as I nodded to Maksym.

"Hold still," I said. Unnecessary, really. But I wanted them to have some kind of warning. Especially considering I had no idea what cutting them off would do to them.

Maksym nodded once, abruptly, the line of werewolves bracing themselves as if expecting a lot of pain.

I hoped they'd be pleasantly surprised.

chapter twenty five

Galleytrot went first, his earth power tied to the chaos of the Wild Hunt, the song of the end of the world humming around him. I watched him create cracks in the hold of the bonds between, breaking them apart with the soaring vibrations of the Wild's music.

They werewolves shuddered as a whole, Maksym's eyes widening, but I gestured for them to stay put.

"Phase one," I said. "My turn."

Galleytrot observed as I allowed my sorcery to explore the last bond, the one crushing the souls of the werewolves. I knew then if I couldn't break it, they would remain slaves to the Czar forever.

Damn it, I sent to the big hound as I saw the truth, how tightly they were held. No way could I free them with just sorcery, or any of my other magicks on their own for that matter. *I need to use my creation power.*

He grunted and sighed. *I concur*, he sent after examining the remaining bond. *This will have to wait. But you must shield them, to keep them safe, if you expect them to be of use to you when you confront their master.*

Got it. Thanks, big guy. I hugged him mentally and he embraced me back, the thrum of earth power reminding me of Liam.

I'm watching over him, Galleytrot sent as though reading my thoughts. *Be safe, Syd.*

Our connection faded and I sagged a little as I refocused on Maksym.

"Okay," I said. "Here's the deal. Your individual bonds are broken." The werewolves nodded, most smiling. Not ready to turn on me yet. Wicked. "But," I said, "there's a problem."

Silence and grimness. Nice. But then again, they had to have trust issues after centuries of being used and abused, and I hardly blamed them.

"The sorcery that made you is keeping you hostage." There was no way I could show them. "In order to break it, I need full access to my magic."

"Then do so," Maksym said. Ordered.

Hold on a freaking minute. I closed the gap between us, temper flaring, jabbing him in the chest with one finger. He was so startled by my reaction to his bossy pants attitude, he backed up a pace, eyes huge.

"Listen," I said. "I'm doing my freaking best here,

okay?" I glared around at the werewolves, seeing their distrust fade, replaced with guilty looks. "But I have other problems besides you all. So, here's the deal. You come with us, I protect you from the Czar. And when we kick his ass, I free you when I'm able to do so."

Maksym hesitated, but I jabbed him again.

"My one and only offer," I said. "Don't push it."

My demon chuckled as the werewolf nodded.

I'm so proud, she sent.

Oh, shut it, I sent back.

Piers took my hand as I stepped away from Maksym. "Now," I said. "Where's the Czar?"

The big werewolf's face hardened, eyes sparking with anticipation. "I can lead you there," he said, guttural voice full of fury and heavy with his accent. "With pleasure."

Our werewolf escort formed up around us as I followed Maksym across the room, leaving the dead sorcerers behind.

"That was close," Piers whispered in my ear.

"Story of my life," I whispered back. "Give me a hand, would you?" I reached for him, my sorcery touching the edge of his. "We need to shield them from the Czar so he can't use them against us."

Piers nodded, his magic flowing into mine easily, as though he'd done something like this before. I flinched at the sharing, feeling like he was suddenly in my space. The emptiness of our mutual power was gone as his being joined with mine.

My, he sent, voice rich and deep as it echoed inside me. *What a lovely soul you have.*

Heat rushed to my cheeks as his power stroked me in places he really shouldn't have been. I slapped him abruptly, though not harshly, and did my best not to grin as he laughed and retreated with reluctance.

Focus, I sent. *Like this.* I showed him the webbing network of shielding I'd adopted so many years ago, during the days I hated magic. Now adapted to my sorcery, it formed a powerful net around myself and, with his help, the werewolves.

I could feel I'd impressed him, heard his low mental whisper of admiration. And wouldn't you know, Piers was a fast learner. Within seconds, a hard shell of sorcery surrounded us. Yes, I could have done it myself, but I needed to be able to defend us with my other magicks when the time came and having Piers there for support meant I could let him take on the bulk of the focus to keep the shield in place.

His mind shuddered as I pulled back and let him support the network, still feeding him power.

Sydlynn Hayle, he whispered in my mind, *I worshipped you before. But now, I'm absolutely in awe.*

Smarty pants, I sent. *Just hold the shape and we'll be fine.*

You think I'm joking, he sent before falling silent.

Maksym led us in a stomping charge through the

palace, out of the wing we were in and into more lived-in sections, bright with light and rich with wealthy accoutrement. A few human servants ran before us, terror on their faces, but we didn't encounter any more werewolves or their horrible sorcerer handlers.

It wasn't until we burst through a large door I realized where he'd taken us. But, to my frustration, the Czar wasn't in his throne room. The huge room echoed hollow with the sound of our marching feet as I stomped my way to the base of the throne dais and spun on Maksym with a scowl.

"Now where?"

He shook his head, shoulders stooping. "He should be here," he said. "He is always here."

The other werewolves nodded, muttered in Ukrainian.

Okay, so we had to do it the hard way. I reached out around me, siphoning off a little sorcery to tie into my demon, vampire and Sidhe power, searching for the Czar. The place was gargantuan, but it was faster to skim using my mind than to tromp our way physically around the acres of property.

After a thorough search of the palace, I came up empty.

All but for the black zone.

"Could they be hiding in the prison area?" I thought of Charlotte. I should have gone after her first.

Maksym shook his head. "No, not there. If he is not in the palace, he has fled."

A soft cheer of victory rose from the werewolves, but I wasn't joining them in their happiness. I'd left far too many enemies behind to raise havoc later and refused to do so this time.

As my magic slowly retreated, I felt the subtle touch of someone I did know. But not on the main level of the building. Underground. I latched onto the whisper of Charlotte's soul through the fluttering black goop, which had weakened for whatever reason, allowing part of her through. My body jerked in response to the discovery.

"What's down there?" I jabbed at the floor beneath my feet, remembering the sight of the fallen weres and sorcerers in the hall Piers destroyed even as Charlotte's presence winked out before coming back into my awareness again.

"Tunnels." Maksym spun and strode off. "Of course, the passageways. This way."

"Not this time." I reached for the veil and tore it open. "There's a faster route from A to B."

The werewolves shuddered at the sight of the glowing amber opening even as Ahbi's power shrieked at me.

Too late. A massive surge of power erupted behind me, slamming me in the back and driving me to my knees. That same power wrapped around me, jerked me backward as Piers's hold on my hand tightened and

Maksym lunged for me.

Flare of blue, fast, lightning fast, too quick for my egos or I to respond. Sudden icy cold as I fell forward on my hands and knees in the snow.

Turned with a snarl and a ball of fire at the ready to find Gwendolyn and Finlay glaring back at me.

"You two," I snarled, "had better back the hell off before I do something permanent to make you."

Finlay's power swelled around him, chest puffing out as blue magic flared. "Try it."

Gwendolyn pressed her hand to his arm, pulling him back, her pretty face filled with distress. "You must stop," she said, to both of us. I stood, still burning with demon fire, Piers beside me, a pool of blackness surrounding us. He still had the shield up. Good boy.

"To hell with that," I said. "Your Council has allowed another magic race to be enslaved for centuries." I cracked a fresh whip of demon fire into a bank of crusted white, a cloud of steam rising as the snow melted in a rush. "Centuries." Shaking? Check. Ready to tear someone a new one? Check. Didn't care who that someone was?

So. Close. To. Check.

"Please," Piers spoke up. "Listen to her. To us. The Steam Union has been asking you to intervene. But nothing has been done and now that same race is in great danger."

Gwendolyn hesitated while Finlay scowled. I was beginning to wonder if the young Enforcer had another expression.

"You're coming with us," he said. "To the border of our territory. And you're going home."

"I hate to repeat you," I shot back. "But try it."

His whole body twitched, broad face bright red. "You're lucky we don't arrest you."

"I wouldn't advise attempting it," Piers said with humor in his voice. Where he could find the funny in this situation was beyond me. Charlotte was moving further and further away, her presence still flickering as though the shielding around her failed from time to time. I had to go after her before the Czar realized she was exposed and sealed her off where I couldn't find her.

But the second I reached for the veil, Finlay's power lashed out and shut me down. I snarled and drew back my demon power as she roared in rage, but just couldn't bring myself to hurt him.

Damned conscience. I really had to do something about it.

"Arrest us if you want," I said while Piers glanced at me with raised eyebrows and whispered, "Us?" "But at least have the guts to help the werewolves who live in *your* territory." I prodded them both with the image of the handler whipping the weres into transforming. "*Your* responsibility." Another shot of Charlotte, spirit broken, the controlling collar around her neck. "*Your* duty."

Even Finlay backed down, head dropping, and though his scowl remained, it was less antagonistic and more hurt.

"We will come with you." Gwendolyn shook her head at her partner when he glared at her in shock. Had to say he wasn't the only one. Had I really gotten through to her at last? "Sydlynn is correct, my friend. We've allowed ourselves to follow a false leader for too long and you know it." He grumbled while my heart leaped, but he didn't argue. Gwendolyn turned to me. "But you will allow us to deal with it, and you will follow our orders."

Whatever helped her sleep at night. "Let's go." I reached for the veil again.

Allowed my demon to take over the long string of cursing I kept inside as Finlay blocked me.

"Show me where to go," he said. "I'll take us."

I rolled my eyes and sighed. Classic, but what other expression would fit such stubbornness?

Whatever.

Even as Finlay reached for my mind, I felt Charlotte's spike of fear and knew we were out of time. I threw the image at him, the one I managed to fish from her frantic mind, saw some kind of podium, as ornate as the palace, in a giant room. With a cross over the back wall.

A cross? They were in a church?

Oh. My. Swearword.

"Hurry the hell up," I said as Finlay's power wrapped around Piers and me. "The bastard is about to marry her."

chapter twenty six

I leaped from the flare of blue magic, out of Finlay's reach, storming down the massive central aisle of the chapel. Um, church. Yikes. Cathedral? The place was massive, just past the outer edge of the palace grounds, full of stained glass depicting religious scenes. But I didn't have time to admire the artwork.

Not while Charlotte knelt at Yure Danko's feet with him smirking down on her.

"Get away from her!" My roar echoed through the place, my demon backing my rage, Shaylee shaking the ground, the pressure of our collective anger shattering some of what was probably priceless glass.

Boo freaking hoo.

I was so tightly in tune with Charlotte I almost missed the sight of Raoul and Oleksander, groveling at Vasyl's side. The Czar's second in command watched my approach with cool calculation while I jabbed my finger at him.

"Go tell Liander Belaisle I'll be seeing him soon." Prod.

The bald sorcerer flinched.

And check mate. Gotcha.

The Czar didn't seem worried as I stomped my way closer. In fact, he seemed eager.

Too eager. I stopped in my tracks, let my sorcery reach out. Felt the werewolves hiding in the pews, their guns aimed and ready.

Bastard. I'd had enough.

Yure looked up over my shoulder and addressed Gwendolyn and Finlay. "We demand you remove this person," he flicked his fingers in my direction, "from our property."

I gaped in absolute shock at his arrogance before slowly pivoting on one booted foot to stare at the pair. Gwendolyn bit her lower lip while Finlay wavered.

No they would *not*.

"Sydlynn." Gwendolyn shrugged, hands open. "I'm sorry. We can't interfere unless a law is being broken."

I spun back and pointed at Charlotte, her father. Her grandfather. "Are you freaking kidding me?"

Finlay had the sense to look uncomfortable when he spoke. "The werewolves are his property," he said. "And he has every right to do with them as he chooses."

So much for them coming to help the enslaved and downtrodden.

"When people become property," I snarled, "witch law has failed."

They both blanched, Gwendolyn's cheeks as pale as a vampire.

"Why did you even bother?" My hiss of rage hurt my throat.

Neither of them spoke. There was nothing to say. They were either with me or against me. On the side of right or getting out of my way.

I heard the ceremony behind me start up again, felt Charlotte's fear turn to dejection and resignation.

No. Not in a million freaking years. No.

I was so done.

With a blast of spirit magic, I shoved the pair of witches back toward the exit. They weren't prepared for the attack, clearly, not from the stunned look on their faces. They bodily impacted the doors, flinging them open. I pushed so hard they fell out of the building before I slammed the way shut behind them and sealed the wood together with a shot of earth magic.

I spun on Piers who grinned at me like this was funny. A snap of power drove the smirk from his face and got his attention.

Keep. Them. Out.

I turned away from him before he could answer and

faced the altar. Reached for Shaylee who sang her joy as she dove beneath the earth and exploded outward.

I'd never been in the middle of an earthquake before. Sure, I'd felt her shake my world, rattle some things. Break a few people. But never an all-out, no holds barred, rip roaring ground splitting.

My magic held me steady, bubble of power thrown out around me as the ceiling groaned and fell, chunks soaring down in slow motion to crush pews to powder. The hidden werewolves screamed in terror, running for their lives as the Czar snarled and created a shield of his own. Around himself.

I've never hated anyone so much in my life. Not Ameline, not Liander Belaisle. That one act of absolute selfishness drove Yure Danko to the depths of my hit list, right below cockroaches and mosquitoes.

I stretched myself thin to protect the werewolves, but I did it. Threw everything I had into it while Shaylee shook and shook.

And shook.

The crisp winter air finally stopped her, as my shivering broke our concentration. When I released the shields around the others and pulled back to my own personal space, I found myself standing in an open channel, the church a pile of rubble around me. I had no doubt the palace behind us suffered terrible damage as well, but that wasn't my problem.

No, my problem stood, untouched and still grinning, at the other end of the empty aisle, waving at the dust cloud now able to settle around us.

He turned and, with deliberation, gestured for the attending official, likely one of his own sorcerers, to resume the ceremony.

"Charlotte!" I screamed her name as I sliced at the power holding her. "Say no! That's all you need to do and I'll finish taking this place apart."

She turned her head, met my eyes. "I don't have a choice," she said. "You know what that feels like, Syd. Don't you?"

Oh, hell. "You do have a choice," I said, walking closer now the werewolves were more interested in running from me than they were shooting me. "If you've learned anything from me, you should know there's always a choice."

"They own my people." She raised her shoulders and dropped them again. "They will own us forever."

"That's a lie." I glared at the Czar even as he laughed at me.

"No," he said. "You are the liar. Our people made them." He grabbed a fistful of Charlotte's hair and jerked her closer to him, her face pressed against his crotch. Horrible, horrible anger burst from my gut and up my chest as he went on. "And there's nothing you can do to change that."

"Let." I slammed power into him, not caring if it was Sidhe or demon or vampire or sorcery. "Her." Again and again, I pummeled him until he staggered back, hand dropping. "Go." One last hit and he grunted, blood bursting from his nose.

Rage flared in his own eyes, finally. He wiped at the blood with one hand, lips curved back, eyes bulging. "I will kill you for that!"

"Don't you mean, 'we'?" Way to prove you're a just an ordinary douchenozzle, dude.

Insanity joined his rage as he spluttered, spit flying from his mouth. He pulled himself together as Charlotte leaned back, eyes locked on mine. With his focus broken, I managed to cut open the bubble of sorcery around her and reach her inner mind at last.

You chose me once, I sent, frantic now to get through to her as her dull eyes told me I was losing her despite my need to pull her closer. *You chose to come back for me. Remember?* Vague recognition lit her gaze. Spluttered like a flame. Died. *And I failed you.* She tried to argue then, but I cut her off. *It's my turn this time, Charlotte. I'm choosing you, don't you understand? I choose you right back.*

Hope, just a flare of it, but enough. *The bond is broken,* she sent. *There's nothing we can do.*

I don't know what it feels like. I wrapped her in my power while the Czar, now aware of the contact, tried to shove me out. *Show me. And I'll do everything I can to rebuild what we lost.*

She hesitated. Only a moment, but long enough Yure's sorcery managed to find an edge and push. But he was too late.

I felt it, the soft kiss of promise, the way the werewolf bond gave a shard of soul from one to the other, creating a connection so profound, so close, they would die without their bonded. Love, family, protection, commitment. All of those and more wrapped up in werewolf power. Their greatest gift and their downfall all in one simple act of giving.

Just as he shoved me out, I felt Charlotte touch me, hold onto me. And together, my power feeding her wolf, we remade the bond.

It sparked along the edges of the bubble holding her captive, burned it away like a fire on a dry patch of grass. The Czar fell back with a cry of fear, almost staggering into Vasyl who pushed him away with disgust on his face. I noted it, but didn't focus on him, not while Charlotte's whole body tensed. Relaxed. Magic pulsed over her, fed by my various magicks. I felt her, clearly, much more clearly this time. Because the bond was no longer one-sided. My vampire, Sidhe, demon and sorcery all linked with her, giving to her as she had given to us.

Charlotte stood in a rush, roaring her joy and her freedom into the bitter cold night sky to the howling counterpoint of her people.

chapter twenty seven

As Yure gaped, I let him feel what I'd done, what Charlotte and I accomplished. Together. No master, no bonded. Equals.

"Impossible," he whispered, the sound carrying in the cold night air.

"Not so much," I grinned at him. "Now, let her go." I glanced at Raoul and Oleksander, both watching me with burning eyes as I faked a thoughtful expression and tapped my chin with one finger. "Come to think of it, I want all the werewolves," I said. "How does that work for you?"

I only had a second to gloat as the Czar stared, unable to comprehend I'd beaten his delusions of godhood. This time I was ready for the burst of witch magic overhead, expected it long before now, to be honest. I was just grateful Applegate waited long enough for me to free

Charlotte before showing up to blast me one.

I wasn't disappointed. She burst into view, surrounded by Enforcers, power crackling around her in a halo of fire.

"COVEN LEADER HAYLE." Her voice boomed through the darkness. I'm sure they heard her in Siberia. "YOU ARE UNDER ARREST. COME QUIETLY OR BE SUBDUED."

Yure's smirk slowly returned. He had the nerve to cross his arms over his chest, resting them on the round of his belly under his heavy robes, looking all satisfied. And toad like.

We'd see about that.

"Council Leader Applegate." I kept my tone light, but firm. "What are your charges?"

She landed on the ground with a thud, vibrating with anger. "I warned you," she snarled, more beast than witch, "if you broke the law, I'd make sure you paid the price."

"I've broken no laws." I gestured around us. "Feel for yourself."

She did. Boy, did she. She searched every blessed inch of the place, my family magic snickering softly to itself as she hunted for traces of witch magic. Blood power. Maji.

Came up empty.

Hell yeah.

"As you are now aware," I said, adding a nice dose of

sarcasm, "I've done nothing but follow your rules since arriving in Europe."

She grunted, gestured around her. "You call this," her voice shook, "following the rules?"

Well, it was rather spectacular. "An earthquake," I said, radiating innocence. I was a terrible liar, true, but this wasn't a lie. "Tragic, isn't it?"

"A localized earthquake," she grated between clenched teeth, "that brought down one of the treasured historical buildings of this region."

"I know," I said, pressing one hand to my chest. "Just horrible. You have my condolences on your loss."

I shouldn't have been prodding her. I knew I was asking for more trouble. But I just couldn't bring myself to behave.

"And your invasion of this territory?" Applegate's eyes shone with satisfaction. "You are unwelcome here, Hayle." I caught a flicker over her shoulder, saw Gwendolyn and Finlay watching, the young witch biting her lip again. "My people were specifically told you were to be escorted off the Czar's property."

Tattle tales.

"Council Leader." Piers stepped slightly past me, letting go of my hand as he did. "Coven Leader Hayle had nothing to do with this invasion." He shrugged. "This has been all my doing and I take full responsibility."

She scowled at him. "You're young Piers," she said.

"Eva's son."

He nodded. "I am. And, as Steam Union, I am outside your purview."

She didn't like that. Not one little bit.

I met Charlotte's eyes as she strode the distance between us. "As the representative of the werewolf nation," she said, addressing Applegate who spun slowly to stare at my werefriend, "I request freedom from the Black Souls and the right to be called our own people."

Go. Charlotte.

Yure choked, lunged for her. "Never," he shrieked. "You're mine!"

Charlotte spun and hit him in the middle of the chest. Not hard. At least, it looked like no more than a love tap. But he went down in a gasping heap.

Calm, almost serene, she stood over him, my magicks rippling around her.

"We will be free," she said. "Even if I have to kill each and every one of your sect in order to ensure my race's liberation." Chilling, how sweetly she spoke, light and full of life while she threatened his extermination.

I was just glad she was on my side.

Applegate knew she was losing control of the situation. I could see the fury working through frustration and hate on her face. Correction, the Brotherhood had to know. Because I could see from the twisting emotions rippling past her eyes she had no intention of letting this pass.

I didn't give her a chance to speak first, instead pointing at Yure who still fought to regain his wind at Charlotte's feet.

"You purposely harbor a criminal in your territory," I said. "One who preys on normals and magical races alike. And autonomous laws aside, it is your responsibility to protect and defend your people from the likes of him." I gave him my own little prod. Right in the place Charlotte hit him. Heard him groan, turned away as he puked up his guts.

Charlotte's grin and offer of a high-five told me she knew exactly what I'd done through the mutual magic we now shared. I slapped her open palm with my own smile.

So nice to have her back.

Margaret Applegate looked like she was about to explode brain matter all over me. It took her a full thirty seconds to pull her crap together, a long and very telling half a minute in which the gathered Enforcers shifted, uncomfortable and uneasy.

Maybe they were finally seeing what was happening to their leader. And would do something about it. Or, maybe, like at home, they would just follow orders as per usual.

Not my problem. At least, not yet.

"Sydlynn Hayle," Applegate finally gasped out as she clutched her own chest as though in pain. "You have poked your nose in where it doesn't belong for the last time."

The air next to me shuddered into shadow just before Sunny, poised and elegant, emerged from the darkness to stare down Applegate. I felt the rapid approach of dawn—holy, had it really only been one night?—and knew she had little time. Even so, she seemed nonchalant as she, Uncle Frank beside her, came to me and kissed both of my cheeks as though Applegate wasn't even there.

"My child," she said, stressing the word in her clear voice. I knew it carried to every pair of ears gathered near. "You're done here?"

"Not quite," I grinned. "Just another minute, great queen."

"Very well." She glanced at Applegate. "I'd hate to think one of my vampires was being treated less than kindly. Or was having trouble for no reason." She fluttered her fingertips at Applegate. "I would have to take appropriate action were that the case."

How did she know to come and rescue me? I had my answer when I caught sight of Isabelle hovering behind Uncle Frank and grinned.

The young vampire beamed back.

I thought Margaret was struck speechless by fury before. I had no idea someone's face could turn that color.

"Since Sydlynn is a member of my family," Sunny pronounced in her precise voice, "she is, naturally, immune to witch law." Said with contempt. And just enough pity the Enforcers twitched again at the implication they were beneath her.

I loved Sunny so much.

"There's the issue of Yure Danko," I said to the vampire queen. She nodded, grave.

"Indeed," she said. "I've been meaning to deal with him personally." He had finally managed to gain his feet, backing away a step as Sunny turned her gorgeous face toward him. "If you will not take care of this smudge of filth," she returned her attention to Applegate, "I will."

I was about to hug her when the air on the other side of me tore wide, gaping amber fire, and, to my utter shock, a towering demon emerged.

I knew her, so it was all good. But still. Who told my sister I needed help?

Meira had aged well beyond her thirteen years, matured by her time spent on Demonicon and exposure to a particularly horrible strain of the power-boosting nectar. I had to admit, even I was nervous as she strode through the veil, dressed in full demon garb, her long, black curls in ornate spirals hanging almost to her platform boots. Amber eyes flared with fire, black horns shining in the light coming from behind her.

Ahbi's magic hugged me, practically bouncing in glee

as Meira spoke.

"WHO DARES ARREST A PRINCESS OF DEMONICON?" The air shook with the power of my sister's voice, boosted with her magic. Meira swept to the right, showing the gap in the veil even as Ahbi's power turned me around. I heard the distinct sound of my grandmother giggling even as I gaped at the ranks of soldiers lined up in the Parade outside the Seat. A demon army waiting to march through and crush all opposition. Dad pulled a similar stunt when Mom was on trial and, I had to admit, it was an impressive threat.

Empty. But impressive.

Applegate spluttered. "You wouldn't dare."

Meira covered the ground between them in two strides, towering over the round woman while her Enforcers had collective fits of fear, power reaching for her. Power Ahbi held back. My sister loomed, glaring her rage at the Council Leader. "I would."

I think Applegate believed her. Hell, I believed her, even though I knew now it was an impossibility. Those demon soldiers wouldn't be able to cross without effigies to fill. Still.

Applegate didn't know that.

I couldn't help the growing smile on my face, the warmth filling me despite the freezing temperatures, as my family came to my rescue.

How freaking awesome.

But the show wasn't over yet, not by a long shot. Just past Applegate, under the hovering Enforcers, a black hole formed, opened. I felt Piers stiffen, heard him say, "Bollocks," before a tall, stunning woman with short blonde hair and a stern expression walked through. Followed by a dozen others, all in gray long coats.

She caught Piers's eye and sighed. He shrugged at her, winked.

Applegate spun on the woman I now assumed was his mother and proved me right.

"Southway!" She fixed her rage on the Steam Union leader as Eva Southway took in the scene. "I'm holding you equally responsible for this mess."

Her gray eyes, the eyes she gave her handsome offspring, met mine. "My son," she said, heavily stressing the term, "may be misguided," in mom speak she was going to turn him into something green and slimy when he got home, "but his convictions are unbroken." She nodded once, sharply. "And I give him my full endorsement. The stain of the Black Souls is one the Steam Union has long meant to erase. Now," she brushed past Applegate, "if you will please leave this property, my people will deal with our business." She fixed Applegate with one raised eyebrow as she looked back over her shoulder at the Council Leader. "Since you are invading my magick's purview."

I loved her already.

And, to be honest, I was half expecting the Sidhe to make an appearance after all this. Was a little breathless from the fun I was having. Yes, I know. It shouldn't have been fun. But it was.

It really, really was.

After all, it was usually me, alone, standing my ground while the bad guys ran. Having a backup choir of assorted powers was the most amazing thing I'd ever experienced.

Giddy, I held my breath, waiting.

No Sidhe made an appearance. Nope, not them.

But there was one final player who still had her cards to lay out on the table.

So I wasn't really all that shocked when the air over my head split in two in a sunburst of blue fire and my mother burst through.

chapter twenty eight

Nice of you to make the party, I sent as she settled on the other side of Sunny. Pender and a large group of Enforcers remained afloat, facing off with the European guard. Things could get ugly really fast, but for some reason I wasn't feeling stressed about it.

I guess I really didn't think the Brotherhood would risk a confrontation with so much firepower on my side. And the fact I was surrounded by those who loved me made a huge difference, when Applegate was pretty much on her own.

Not for the first time, I wondered where her Enforcer Leader, Elliot, had gone. Had a sudden sick feeling about him.

Hoped I was wrong.

"You've brought our two territories to the edge of war." Mom was in Applegate's face so fast the woman retreated, Meira stepping away to give our mother her kick at the can. Mom turned to her, smiled up at my sister like nothing was going on and patted her hand. "Hi, sweetie."

Meira bent and kissed Mom's cheek. "Hi, Mom."

Surreal.

Their simple exchange had an amazing effect on Applegate. She froze, face suddenly slack, as though her controllers had no idea how to take the situation they found their puppet in. If I ever had a scrap of doubt the Brotherhood owned her, it was gone with that obvious lack of soul staring out of her eyes.

And her Enforcers saw it. A ripple of despair went through them. I reached out to them, felt their power. They remained clean, all of them, not a taint of sorcery to be found. But Applegate was a lost cause.

Mom, I can try to free her, I sent. *If there was ever a good time...*

She hesitated.

Too long, it turned out.

Applegate twitched, face a sunken mask of absolute hate, eyes crawling with black. The Czar must have seen she'd lost, because he chose that unfortunate moment to speak up.

"We demand—"

He didn't get a chance to finish. Applegate spun on him with a snarl and extended one hand. Her power wrapped around his throat and squeezed, so hard and so fast no one could act quickly enough.

Not that I wanted to save him or anything. But I would have liked to have been spared the splintering sound his spine made as she crushed his neck. I couldn't help but wonder as I forced my mind to detach from the popping, snapping soundtrack of his death if the Brotherhood were behind this particular execution or if it was just Applegate's build-up anger finding a place to outlet.

Belaisle. Had to be.

Which made me question what Yure may have known that could have helped me.

Too late now. Damn it. But at least I'd saved the werewolves from a fate worse than Yure Danko.

"Father!" Isabelle's broken cry bit through the night air as she rushed forward, held back only when Piers gently caught her and kept her from reaching the dying Czar.

Yes, he was a scumbag. But he was her dad. I got it.

Didn't like it. But I got it.

The gathered sorcerers of his sect wavered, cried out, sinking to their knees to weep into their hands at the loss of their leader. My quick visual search for Vasyl turned up nothing, though. Cut and run. Back to his masters, I supposed.

Let him go. This one was a victory for the good guys.

I just wished I was there to see Liander's face when his little viper came crawling home.

The whole place fell silent, the whistle of the wind the only sound. That and the solid thud of the Czar's dead body as Applegate released him to crash to what remained of the floor.

Piers finally let Isabelle go, the young vampire falling to her knees at Yure's side. She didn't touch him, simply hugged herself and rocked forward and back while the soft keening of the werewolves marked his passing. It grew from a hum to a bellow to a roar as they threw up their arms and howled their joy into the darkness.

Applegate turned back to me, her hate still alive and well, though her little execution seemed to have pulled her under control. She didn't speak until the last of the werewolves fell silent again, but her message was expected. "You are no longer welcome in Europe," she said. "And will be escorted out of my territory."

"No," I said, feeling the magic around me, my mother, sister, Sunny, the Steam Union, all pushing against her. "I'm not going anywhere. You have no say over what I do and you know it. Follow your own laws for once, Applegate."

The woman's shriek of frustration cut through me as she lurched into the air, gathered up her Enforcers and vanished in a blast of blue flame.

Most of her Enforcers. A handful remained behind.

And my babysitters.

Figured.

I chose to ignore them, knowing Pender would hold them off if necessary and hugged Mom. She kissed me softly before I squeezed Meira and Sunny. Uncle Frank. Turned to Piers, who offered his hand to his mother.

"Sydlynn Hayle," he said. "May I introduce Eva Southway?"

A slim girl hugged Piers as his mother shook my hand, her power touching mine out of courtesy. I fought off the immediate stab of jealousy at the sight of him hugging the thin, pretty thing, trying not to let his cheating bastard status ruin things for me. I was so pissed for her I wanted to punch him in his happy place.

"I wish I could say it's a pleasure," Eva said. "At least, the circumstances."

I nodded, refusing to look at Piers. "Me, too." I said. "Maybe we can arrange a more formal intro once this is over."

She smiled, just a little. "I look forward to it," she said before bowing her head to Mom, Sunny and Meira.

I turned, forgetting the fact I was as guilty of kissing someone other than my significant other, and went looking for Charlotte. Found her and the werewolves coming to gather around the fallen form of the Czar, his own people shrinking from them as they herded the few sorcerers of the sect into the center with their dead

227

master.

One more thing to do before this was over.

I joined my friend over the body of her fallen master. Charlotte looked up at me, smiling, really smiling, her eyes full of tears, one crystallizing on her cheek in the cold. Only then did I remember the frigid temperature and begin to shiver, though it was at that moment I understood I really wasn't cold. It was in my head.

Sharing the bond with Charlotte had created another new pathway inside me, freeing me from common discomfort as much as our link liberated her from the Czar.

Another step closer to being full maji. One more benefit of membership, I supposed.

"My people." She turned to them as Raoul came and hugged her, Oleksander embracing her, too, kissing the top of her head. "It's time we were free forever."

They rumbled their unhappiness, some looking terrified, others clutching their guns to their chests as though they couldn't bear to be parted with the life they knew. I was sure she and her family would have a big job on her hands. The training of centuries of servitude wouldn't be erased overnight, no matter her wishes to the contrary.

"Trust in your princess," Oleksander said. Smiled at me, blue eyes full of hope. "Trust in Sydlynn Hayle."

I glanced down at the small group of sorcerers and

realized just how few there had been all along. How twisted and horrible they were, their faces the same, some distorted by inbreeding. And when I looked up again at the growing crowd of looming werewolves, I realized how thin their thread of slavery really was.

Time to break it.

Charlotte must have been sharing my thoughts still through the power between us, because she took my hand.

"We have been too long under the control of those without honor." She wiped at the tear on her face, the piece of ice falling free. "It is time to live our own lives, to make our own way. A way built on the principles we choose."

I nodded while the werewolves did, too, hanging on her every word while Oleksander beamed in pride.

"Will you help us?" I'd never seen her look so happy, so much like just a beautiful young woman without the accustomed hard shell she usually wore. "Will you free us from them?"

"I will," I said. "But I can only break the first bond at this point."

Maksym grunted and spoke up. "She did as she promised," he said to his pack. "She freed us of our individual bonds to them." He spit on the ground, the beautiful tile crystallizing with frost from its exposure to the open air. His eyes met mine. "We are ready to be free of all constraints."

Finally, murmuring hope, the shedding of guns, a hundred pairs of eyes staring at me while, through Charlotte, I felt hundreds more out there, in the world, working for sorcerers they despised.

Their handlers were about to get a very unhappy wakeup call.

I turned to Mom and the others, seeing Meira perk as though she knew what I was thinking.

"I need your help." They gathered around, Sunny and Uncle Frank despite the threat of coming morning. Piers and Eva, Mom, Meira, even while the few Enforcers Applegate left behind tried to break us up.

Pender took care of things above while I connected with the others.

I need to use my maji power, I sent. *But in order to do it, I need to act through you to disguise what I'm doing.*

Mom didn't hesitate. Neither did Meira or Sunny. Eva looked confused and alarmed. But when Piers freed himself from the girl at his side and reached for my hand while my jealousy twinged despite my focus, she slapped it away.

Tell us what you need us to do, she sent, mental voice as crisp as her spoken one.

Just let me in, I sent. *I'll do the rest.*

You're hoping this works. Leave it to my vampire to douse me with a splash of cold reality.

I am. I didn't have a Sidhe power to work through, but since Applegate couldn't access the magic of the Fey, I wasn't worried about her poking holes in my story.

No, I needed witch magic. But using the others to diffuse my magical scent would go a long way to keeping what I was about to do under wraps.

You hope, my vampire sent again.

Oh, hush, my demon growled at her.

Shaylee's giggle made me grin.

I turned to Charlotte, pushing myself into the magic users behind me even as I spoke. "You want freedom?" I beamed at her as I then reached to her, through her, down the path of her blood to every werewolf alive. "You got it."

chapter twenty nine

I was just funneling my power back out through the others when I felt the whispered touch of maji magic in my mind.

Sydlynn. Iepa, my maji guide/pain in the rear embraced me gently.

Don't tell me this isn't allowed, I snapped at her in auto-defense mode. Because that would be just like her, popping in at the time when happiness was a thread of power away.

She released me, sighed softly. *To the contrary,* she sent. *What you're about to do, the freedom you offer them, is how the werewolves were meant to be.*

Huh? *What do you mean?*

The sorcerers didn't create them, per se, she sent. *Yes, they finished the job, sealed the shifting race to them. But the initial creation was mine.*

You again. I wished I could throttle her. *Why didn't you rescue them?*

I couldn't, she sent. *But you can.*

Why am I so special? Bitter? Naw.

Because you share a bond with one of them, she sent. Had me focus on Charlotte again. *Your black hound friend had the right of it.* She showed me what he did, the quaking of the edges of the bond. *But you need to take it even further.* Instead of earth magic severing a hold, she pushed me deeper, into the very cells of my werefriend. Each one was surrounded by black. *You need to break it at the molecular level. But you can't just leave them unsupported.* She showed me another image, of the cells breaking free and shattering. *They will die.*

Gulp. *Okay, so what, then?*

You replace it. Iridescent light flared around the cells once filmed in darkness.

Whoa, I sent. *I'm not going to be their new Czar.*

You won't be, she sent. *You are simply freeing them from the hold of sorcery. It devours for strength. Instead of it, you're giving them creation magic to sustain them and help them grow to full potential.*

No strings? I didn't think Charlotte would forgive me if she traded one master for another.

None, Iepa sent. *They will be as they were always meant. And will finally develop their own magic.*

Coolio. *Let's do it.*

But she pulled away. *I can only guide you, as always*, she sent. *I have absolute faith you will succeed.* She paused before her power hugged me quickly again. *Be well, Sydlynn Hayle. I will speak to you again soon.*

I wasn't sure if that was a warning things were coming to a head shortly or if there was hope in her voice. Either way, she was gone and I knew better than to chase after her.

Syd. Mom's mind touched mine. *Are you going to do something or are we just going to stand here?*

I shot her a grin. *Iepa moment*, I sent back. *I'm getting to it.*

When I turned back and met Charlotte's eyes, she smiled.

Yeah. I had this handled.

It was easier even than Iepa said, though much more moving than I expected. The moment I released Charlotte's body of the sorcery, my maji power rushed in to repair the damage, seal her cells with power and creative magic. I watched her change on the outside even as my mind saw her shift on the inside, her skin seeming to glow a moment, the rainbow light of my maji power pouring from her for a couple of heartbeats, pulsing in time with her blood, before she returned to normal.

No, not normal. She still glowed, with an inner beauty that came from being free.

Charlotte sobbed and reached for me, hugging me

tight, lips pressing first to my left, then my right cheek. When she let me go, she twirled like a little girl and laughed, wrapping her own arms around her.

"Thank you," she said. Sobered a little. "Can you save them all?"

Only one way to find out.

I reached through her again, using her bloodline to find them one last time, to do for every werewolf as I'd done for Charlotte. It seemed to take forever, my maji power whispering its way across miles, healing, cleansing, freeing. I was so focused on what I was doing, it wasn't until the last werewolf, a continent away, roared in triumph I returned my attention to my physical body.

And found myself held in Piers's arms. My knees quivered as I clutched at him, grateful he held me up.

"Thought you could use a hand this time," he said.

"Thanks." I tested my strength as the werewolves gathered around each other, whispering, hugging, their happiness so vivid my chest tightened. Maybe I was just emotional from what I'd done, or maybe I'd been through so much in the last twelve or so hours, I earned it, but as they quietly celebrated their freedom, I turned my face into Piers's shoulder and wept.

He hugged me, magic and all, not a breath of judgment. Only support and kindness until I snuffled and wiped at my nose, just in time to see Charlotte approaching with a shy smile.

All of her gathered people assembled behind her.

Some of them fell to their knees, their awe and wonder so clear I pulled free of Piers and shook my head.

"You're on your own," I said. "Don't even think about it."

Charlotte laughed as Oleksander stepped forward to mimic her, his beard scratching my face as he kissed my cheeks. "How can we ever repay you?"

Silly werewolf. "You are your own people now," I said. "I have it on very good authority you were always meant to be this way." More awe, some weeping of their own. "Now that you are free, I will make it a priority to have the reproduction ban lifted in North America."

Mom came to my side with a smile. "I can promise that will no longer be an issue."

I loved my mother. "And the offer is open—come visit me sometime and tell me about your own adventures." Be nice to hear about someone else's for a change.

Their magic flowed around them, a hot, churning feeling reminding me of a mix of demon and earth magic. Made sense, considering Charlotte's ability to cross to Demonicon, though in altered form. I suddenly wondered if she went over the veil now, would she be in demon shape?

I also couldn't help but ask myself what I'd helped to bring into the world. As long as they stayed the good guys, things couldn't have turned out better.

Syd, Mom sent, arm going around my shoulders as Piers backed off. We watched Charlotte return to her people, Oleksander pausing to kiss my cheeks one last time before hugging his granddaughter in a bear-like grip and laughing. *You did good, sweetheart.*

I grinned at Mom and shrugged.

All in a night's work for a Hayle, I sent.

I knew trouble was coming but didn't care. It floated down to our level in the form of Gwendolyn and Finlay, who managed to sneak past Pender and confront me.

The young witch was still biting her lip. If she wasn't careful, she wouldn't have one left by the time the sun rose.

"We've been instructed to escort you to our border." At least she wasn't going to call me on the blatant use of maji power I just performed. Still, her words rankled.

Charlotte didn't give me a chance to defend myself. She pulled free of her celebrating people and crossed the distance in three long strides, pushing her way into Gwendolyn's face. Charlotte's echoing growl made my teeth ache, her power flaring around her as her wolf leaped into her eyes.

"Tell your Council Leader," she snarled, "her witches are no longer welcome in our territory." The werewolves roared their approval. "And that Sydlynn Hayle is always welcome." More roaring. They'd wake up half the countryside. "She is my guest. And I will escort her home."

Not much they could say to that. With an apologetic shrug, Gwendolyn returned to the small contingent of Enforcers and, in a flare of blue, they were gone.

And that was how the extended Hayle family kicked ass.

Boo-ya.

chapter thirty

Home. Wilding Springs had never looked so amazing. Early daylight embraced me as I stepped out of the veil and into the dawn-lit kitchen. It only took a second for Shenka to come running, Sassafras bounding at her side, his furry body leaping into my arms as she hugged him between us.

A cup of coffee at the table later and the pair were sitting back with headshakes and snarky comments about troublemakers.

It was actually kind of funny.

"Who knew Sydlynn Hayle aspired to be Creator." Sass swiped his tongue over one paw before rubbing his nose, amber eyes sparkling with mischief.

"Oh dear," Shenka said, clasping her hands in front of her chest. "I forgot we have greatness among us." She slid to one knee at my side, looking up at me with fake adoration while trying to keep a straight face.

I was surrounded by smarty-pants.

I swatted at her, giggling while Sassafras laughed.

"Pick on me all you want," I said. "But it was pretty cool."

Shenka relented, taking her seat to squeeze my hands. "Charlotte must be over the moon."

The second I thought of my werefriend, my heart constricted. I missed her already.

A quick shower did me wonders, though, as I stood under the super hot water, heat I barely felt anymore, I felt sadness creep up. This immortality thing took all the fun out of things. And I really had to get my head out of the cloud of helping Charlotte and back into classes. I had school in a few hours, unbelievable. How was I going to suddenly switch focus from big, massive, life changing back to hum-drum, listen to a lecture?

Oh, right. Been there, done that, burned the cookies.

I'd be fine.

I was just pulling on a fresh pair of jeans when I felt the shadowy darkness of sorcery enter my kitchen. My typical reaction to such an event had worn down from freaking out the Brotherhood attacking to, oh it must be Demetrius. I knew he'd want to hear all about my time with the Steam Union, considering the damaged sorcerer had supposedly begun his magic life with them. But when I entered the kitchen, still toweling my hair, it wasn't wide blue eyes that greeted me, but a pair of pale gray.

Piers sat, one leg crossed casually over the other, a big hand stroking Sassafras's fur while the silly cat purred his head off. I tossed the towel into a chair, touching my wet hair, feeling suddenly self-conscious in my worn denims and raggedy t-shirt, wishing I'd left a few nice things at home and hadn't taken them all to school.

Then sizzled in anger at the fact he'd played me, using our mutual attraction when he had no intention of following through.

Like I had. Yeah, nice argument. Lie to yourself much?

Piers's eyes sparkled as he rose to take my hand, guiding me into the seat next to him, which he first pulled out and then pushed in for me. Weird. And yet, chivalrous enough I had a quiver in some low places that really should be reserved for Liam.

My. Boyfriend. Boy. Friend. Syd.

Sigh.

"Young Master Southway seems quite impressed with you, Sydlynn." Way for Sass to go all formal and stuff. And since when did he have a British accent, even the hint of one? "I told him to wait a little while and get to know you better."

Smartass cat. "I take it you're here for a reason?" It came out snarky for a couple of reasons. We'd just parted ways, after all. Piers left with his mother after convincing the werewolves to allow the Steam Union to take custody of the sect of Black Souls.

I didn't think they'd accept the arrangement. It had taken a few hours of convincing, bartering and badgering, but Eva Southway was eloquent and persuasive. And I think Charlotte finally just wanted the sorcerers of both ilk out of her life so her people could move on.

Knowing they were going to trial and execution probably helped a bit.

The second reason had to do with his girlfriend. And my renewed irritation I'd let him kiss me.

Wanted him to.

Girlfriend hell? Save me a room.

"Mother has sent out some of our people to gather the scattered members of the sect who had werewolves in their possession." He grinned at me, nastiness in that smile. "And a few others the sorcerers forced the werewolves to bond with." I thought of the Dumonts and felt myself smiling, too. "Once all are tracked down, Mother promised to return the weres to Charlotte."

Well, Oleksander, he meant. Charlotte was to be heir, at least from what I overheard of the conversation she had with her grandfather before Mom and Meira left. Sunny and Uncle Frank were forced to flee as dawn approached, long before I left the palace grounds, and I promised to return to Austria that night to catch them up on the whole story.

"Good to know." I could just imagine, after feeling their joy at freedom, what some of the gifted werewolves did to their former masters.

Yeah, yuck. Blood and guts and rending of limbs came to mind.

"It's going to be a big adjustment for them," Piers said, scratching Sass behind one ear while the Persian settled his head into the sorcerer's hand. "They'll need support."

"And they'll have it." I was so glad I trusted my instincts, no matter what Charlotte thought at the time. Family was everything. Which made me then think of his home situation. "Is your mom still mad at you?"

He winced before shrugging. "She's furious," he said. Laughed. "But she's agreed to act, at last. So thank you for that."

"I think you managed that one all on your own." Might as well give him the credit he was due. In the spirit of working together and everything.

Syd. Stop stroking his ego and get on with it. Sheesh.

"I wanted to tell you we now believe you were right about Vasyl Krajnik." Big surprise there. He'd given himself away when I prodded him about Belaisle. "We have been unable to locate him and believe he's run to the Brotherhood for protection."

"Let him," I said. "If this all turns out the way I hope it does, he'll get his eventually."

243

"And if it doesn't?" Piers was only being playful, I could tell. But his words sent a shiver up my spine.

"We'll all be dead," I said, expressionless and cold inside. "So it won't matter, will it?"

Sassafras glared at me with a little hiss before tossing his tail and turning his back. He thudded his way across the table and left in a huff.

Like I'd insulted him directly. So sensitive.

"I'm allowed to be realistic," I called after him.

Piers laughed. "I like your cat," he said.

"I do, too," I said. "Some days."

He leaned toward me, sunlight making his skin glow. "Speaking of being realistic," he said. And kissed me.

Um hum. Heat, the heat I'd been missing from the shower, and tingling, from the tips of my toes to the roots of my hair rolled through me. My right hand cupped the back of his head, pulled him closer while I braced myself with my free hand on his knee. He leaned in, the scents of coffee and mint so delicious I instantly wanted to devour him.

When I pulled away, Piers sighed over my mouth.

Holy. Sydlynn Thaddea Hayle.

Boy. Freaking. Friend.

I took a breath, inhaling his air even as I quivered. "I have a. Um. You know."

"A boyfriend?" Piers laughed deep and soft, still sharing my oxygen. "Yes, I know."

"And you do, too." I paused. "Have one." Another awkward moment. "A girlfriend." Way to have a nerdgirl attack, Syd.

His frown of confusion turned to a low laugh that sent ripples of delight through my body.

"I don't think Clover qualifies," he said, eyes heavy lidded as he leaned in to brush his nose against mine. "You're referring, I believe, to the young woman on my arm last night?"

Blush. "She's not?"

"She's not," he said. "In fact, that would be highly inappropriate considering she's my sister."

Ah. Okay then.

"Why," he said, lips hovering, hot breath setting me on fire. "Jealous?"

Oops.

Damn it.

Piers laughed, stole a quick kiss and backed off. "Which brings us to the realistic part."

"How's that?" Focus. So hard to focus when I just wanted to kiss him again.

"I understand there's a bit of a competition going on," he said. "And witch leadership rules are in effect in a few months."

I was going to kill that damned cat. Skin him and wear his fur for a hat.

If Piers thought his little talk was going to get him

anywhere, he had another damned thing coming—

This time when he kissed me, he didn't hold back. I found myself in his lap, hands wound through his long hair, inhaling him, tasting him while even my demon begged me for just a little more.

I gasped and pulled away, sliding into my seat with some reluctance. "Are you kidding me?"

"I'm very serious," he said. Took my hand and kissed the back of it. "I'm offering myself as a suitor, Coven Leader Hayle. And I hope you'll accept my advances."

Well, since I'd just did the tongue-wrestling match of the century with him, accepting his advances didn't seem to be the issue.

Piers rose before I could come out of my gaping spaz attack and bowed to me.

"I'll see you soon," he said before he formed a black hole with his sorcery and stepped through it.

I waffled between giggling into my hands in near hysteria and kicking myself for being such an idiot.

Like I needed another boy to worry about.

CHAPTER THIRTY ONE

I stood outside the throne room at the palace, trying to figure out what to do with my hands as I forced myself to smile and nod at guests as they passed by. The slim black dress Mom made me wear didn't have pockets, so I caught myself fidgeting between clasping them behind my back and toying with the thin silver band I wore around my thumb as a show of some kind of decoration.

When the invitation to Oleksander's coronation came to me at Harvard a few days ago, I had to say yes. If only for the chance to see Charlotte again so soon. It had been less than a week, but the werewolves made themselves very much at home in the old palace, more and more of them arriving from far-flung shores, free of their captivity.

Mom's smile was much more genuine as she slipped up beside me and took my elbow in one hand.

It will be over soon, she sent as she accepted cheek kisses from a Steam Union member.

The throne room beyond was packed with people, from vampires to sorcerers, witches to werewolves. Someone had managed to hang new doors, since the previous ones were gone thanks to my over-enthusiastic alter egos. I found myself wincing and grinning by turn as I thought about the crazy twelve hours I'd endured, struggling to stay present even while being forced to greet perfect strangers every two seconds.

Eva Southway cracked a smile at me as she glanced over the head of a small couple who practically gushed as they turned to see me. I hugged Nataliya Makosky, nodding and smiling as she babbled at me, then her husband, in her native tongue. It was nice to see her again, despite the circumstances of our first meeting and, when she moved on, it was clear from the brightness of her smile she thought so, too.

You're a celebrity, Eva sent, gray eyes weighing my every move. Why was she watching me like she was waiting for me to make a mistake?

I'm afraid you're mistaken, I sent back. *I'm just a coven leader from America.*

She turned away, Piers firmly held in place next to her. He blew me a kiss while his mother frowned at him.

Made me giggle, in spite of myself.

I don't think Eva Southway likes me, I sent to Mom.

She hugged me as we held our place at the top of the receiving line. Weird setup, as far as I was concerned, but I understood Charlotte's reasoning, having all of us here like this. Even Sunny and Uncle Frank had their spot in the line, Meira on the other side of Mom. A show of solidarity for the werewolves from some of the most powerful people on the plane—and beyond—had to go a long way to cement their right to their own rule.

Do you care if she doesn't like you? Mom's tone was light, but I could tell she was fishing.

Not at all, I sent, just as airy. *Since I'm gathering a list, I figured I'd add her to it.*

Mom laughed in my head. *Syd*, she sent, *I think her dislike—if, in fact, it is dislike—has less to do with what you are and more to do with who you are.*

Sorry? I was getting very tired of being ogled. Double cheek kissed. Looked at with fear and awe. But at least I didn't have Meira's problem. Most of the guests shrieked a little when they were faced with her towering, red-skinned, black-horned stunningness.

I believe the Steam Union leader is weighing your suitability to marry her son. Mom held me still as I tried to whip around and glare at her, pinning me tight with her arm around my waist, her free hand still holding my elbow.

Where did you hear that?

Oh, Syd. She was totally baiting me, her mental voice full of giggles. *You're telling me it's not true?*

No. Comment.

The line was finally done, the last of the invited guests passing through. I glanced around at our little group and felt a shiver of satisfaction as I shoved aside the issue of Piers for now. Because avoiding making decisions was my favorite course of action. Instead, I grinned and caught myself nodding in satisfaction.

Among the crew of us, we could do some serious damage.

And not one of us wondered why Charlotte hadn't invited Margaret Applegate.

Shocking, I know.

Mom released me with a soft kiss on my cheek, taking Uncle Frank's arm as he guided both her and Sunny into the throne room. I let Piers walk ahead of me, his mother watching with her piercing gray eyes, doing my best not to show her she was creeping me out.

Meira brushed past me, winking down at me. She had to wear those damned platform boots that made me feel like a munchkin, didn't she?

Bratski.

It wasn't until she passed through the doors I drew a breath and prepared to follow.

Heard footsteps behind me, the whisper of clothing. Turned.

Was crushed in a very enthusiastic hug. I hugged Charlotte right back, tears squeezing out of my eyes as we rocked and laughed.

"*Я тебе кохаю*," she whispered.

"I love you, too," I whispered back.

Charlotte stepped back, beaming, radiant. Someone had given her an updo that made her shorn hair look long again, makeup tasteful but dramatic. She wore a slim, ivory gown, almost like a bride, the silk floating around her in a cloud of fabric.

"You look gorgeous," I said.

One shaking hand pressed to her pink cheeks. "I'm nervous," she said. "Can you tell?"

So funny, this new Charlotte, with her open smile and sharing of confidence. I shook my head.

"Not at all," I said. "You're a rock."

She stuck out her tongue at me, such a child-like gesture I had to laugh.

"I'm not supposed to be here." She gripped my hands between hers. "But I wanted to see you before the ceremony."

Before she was bound to her people as heir forever.

I refused to be sad. Chose, instead, to be happy and proud. But knowing our days together were really over took a toll, I couldn't deny it. I'd missed her far more than I'd been willing to admit to myself in the last few months. And now that I had Charlotte in my life again, I wasn't sure how I was going to fill the void when she was gone.

Get used to it, Hayle. The older I got, the more

people I was going to lose.

Happy thoughts. Happy.

Charlotte's budding power reached out for me and I embraced it.

"You'll have to learn to control your magic," I said. Sounded like my mother.

"I know," she said. "I'm hoping I can have some help in that department from time to time?"

I grinned. "Anytime."

"Oh, Syd." She hugged me again, voice cracking. "I miss you so much, do you know that?" She pulled away again, dabbing at her eyes and fanning her face to keep from crying. "When we reformed the bond, when I realized it was no longer one-sided, I knew what my people could accomplish. And that they had to be free." She sighed. "That I had to be able to act on my own without you. Being tied to you, as an equal, was the most incredible experience I've ever lived." She shivered in delight, face bright with the memory. "But it had to end so my fellow werewolves could see I was committed not only to my own freedom, but to theirs, to our race's."

I nodded, choked up. Heard the sound of trumpets and knew we were out of time.

She looked over her shoulder, turned back to me, speaking in a rush. "I've thought long and hard over things these last few days. I've realized after everything that happened to me, I need to be with my family." My heart tightened at those words, knowing it was the end for real. Yes, I knew. But she said it. And she had to say it. We both needed to hear it. "I have to keep my family safe, Syd. You taught me that." Her smile woke up again. "There is so much turmoil, the world in such a mess. So much to come... I have to be ready to stand with those I love and do everything I can to save them."

I hugged her quickly, heard fast footsteps approach.

"Sharlotta." Raoul's voice hissed from behind her and we both turned to see him waving for her to come.

Charlotte laughed and kissed my cheek before running to her father, light as a feather. She waved to me as she took his hand and I waved back, turning away so she wouldn't see me cry.

No way was I ruining this for her.

I went looking for my seat next to Mom, the throne room filled to near bursting with chairs, only a narrow way open to the throne dais. I barely noticed the stares from the crowd as I drifted up the aisle, mind churning and heart sore. Mom took my hand as I sat down, squeezed it, but didn't comment.

Good thing. I'm sure I would have burst into tears.

The ceremony was long and complicated and in Ukrainian. I did a lot of standing and sitting down at random intervals when everyone else did. But the time went by in a blur. The only moment that really mattered to me was when Charlotte bent her head to accept her crown.

Saying goodbye was part of life. But this was one of the hardest goodbyes I'd ever had to say.

chapter thirty two

I sat on the edge of Liam's bed, trying to study, failing miserably. He lay beside me, one hand stroking my leg as he read from a textbook. He hadn't pushed me for much information about what I was now calling The Charlotte Incident, and I was grateful. Partially because whenever I thought about my werefriend I either started to cry and couldn't stop or I thought about Piers.

Way worse. Especially considering the company I kept.

Liam finally closed his book over and tried to pull me down beside him. My whole body resisted, to the point I shut my laptop lid and stood up to avoid him.

The hurt look on his face was almost too much.

"What's wrong?" Green glittered in hazel.

"Nothing." I was a record scratched so deep I couldn't come up with another answer to his almost constant question.

"Syd," he said. "You keep saying there's nothing wrong. But you haven't been yourself since you got back from the Ukraine."

Sigh. "I just have a lot on my mind." Wow, nice line, Hayle. Oh, and don't meet his eyes, right. Keep yours on anything but the pain in his. Very classy. "I have to go."

Liam stood, came after me, but I was already slipping on my jacket, halfway out the door before he could reach me.

I stuffed my computer in my bag, struggling with my coat and scarf, though I didn't need them anymore. Weird, just weird. And only added to the craziness of what I was becoming.

When I almost dropped half the contents of my purse onto the ground on the top step outside Liam's dorm, I finally stopped and took my time putting my physical self together while my internal self slowly unraveled.

Do you love him? My vampire spoke gently.

I don't know. I sagged against the stair railing and shrugged. Two normal students walking past me looked at me like I'd lost it.

Maybe I had.

I do, I sent. *But I'm not sure if he's the right one for me. This is so hard.*

It is, she sent. Really helpful. *But we are here for you, to help you make your decision.*

256

Right. *You guys have to live with him too, don't you?* Forgot about that.

We will adore whomever you choose, my vampire sent while my demon grumbled, but finally agreed.

We love you, Syd, Shaylee sent. *And we love Liam.* More demon grumbles. *But if you choose another, that's all right, too.*

But if you do, I get to pick the next one, my demon sent.

We all laughed while I imagined the fiery, brightly burning disaster she'd likely saddle us with.

Syd. Mom's voice cut through the conversation. *Are you nearby?*

I looked down the Yard at Massachusetts Hall. *I can be there in a second.*

No rush, she sent. *But I have dinner ready if you're hungry.*

My stomach chose that exact moment to grumble.

Mom didn't say much as she doled out spaghetti and meatballs, sliding two thick slices of garlic toast onto my plate. The smell was divine and I kept my fingers crossed I would never lose my nose for delicious like I did my sensitivity to cold and hot.

Man, that would suck.

It wasn't until we were almost done, my fork scraping over the last of the sauce on the bottom of my plate, that Mom spoke.

"I wanted you to know how proud I am of how you handled yourself, sweetheart." Mom's blue eyes shone with her smile.

"Thanks, Mom," I said. Sighed and set aside my fork. "I made a mess, but I cleaned it up." Well, mostly. Wasn't much I could do about the shattered ruin of the palace church.

"You did what you had to do and you followed the rules." Mom grinned. "Well, mostly."

A giggle escaped me. "I'm good at mostly."

We clinked glasses in celebration of good enough.

"Margaret's state is an issue," she said, sobering. "Though it appears the Brotherhood are, as of yet, unprepared for war between territories." Mom set down her wine glass and threaded her hands together in front of her. "She's been speaking to the other Council Leaders, but so far no one has taken her side. Which gives me hope they aren't under Brotherhood control."

Good to know. "I had a thought," I said, remembering another friend who had been left behind. "Now that I know Applegate's rules, I can free Sebastian as long as I don't use witch magic."

Mom's continuing hesitation told me nothing had changed, at least for her.

"I worry for him," she said. "But I fear any kind of further prodding might push the Brotherhood past the point of no return. And we can't risk that just yet."

I nodded, frustrated, but knowing she was right.

"This summer will tell us much," Mom said. "And while I know you want to act now, having a world conclave of Councils will give us access to all of the territories. And grant us the opportunity to check all of them together for Brotherhood influence."

"I don't know that we can afford to wait, Mom." I sat back, dinner not sitting so well with me anymore. "What if the Brotherhood is ready to act before conclave happens? That's August. And we're in January." Months. So much could happen in so many months.

"I know," she said. "I really do, Syd. And I've considered other options, such as going to see them individually. But if I do that, the Brotherhood has warning, can act on one while I'm with another." She dropped her hands, cutlery jumping. "And yes, I understand they will see through the conclave call. That they will expect our tactics, know it is our way of examining each of the Councils." She shook her head, long, black hair swinging over her shoulders in glossy curls.

"I could just gather them up and take care of it." Tempting.

"Don't think I haven't considered that option," Mom said with a little smile. "And I'm not even kidding."

Okay then.

"I'm already getting positive responses from the other Councils," Mom said, "despite Applegate's campaign against you." She laughed. "Maybe because of it. I'm sure they are curious to meet you at this point."

Ah, fame. Blerg.

"As long as we're able to hold things together," Mom said. "August will be a telling month."

I nodded, glum. August. Almost three months *after* my birthday. Mom must have known where my mind was, because her magic reached for me, ever so gently.

"How's Liam?"

Gulp.

"Fine," I said, sipping my water. Avoiding her eyes.

Because that would work on my mother.

Um-hum.

"Syd." She reached for my hand, squeezed it. "You know if I could change this law for you, I would."

Shrug. "I guess so."

Mom's chuckle tweaked my temper.

"Believe me," she said. "I know exactly how you feel."

I finally met her eyes. "You loved Dad."

She nodded, gaze far away even as my heart ached for her loss. She really did love him, probably would always pine for him though I hoped she considered dating at some point.

Shiver.

"It wasn't easy making the decision to marry Harry," she said. "Knowing how hard you girls would have it. Especially your sister." She sat back with a sigh, setting aside her napkin, swirling her wine in her glass. The dark red liquid left a pink coating on the crystal. "But I trusted myself, my instincts. And you need to, as well."

"There's just one problem with that advice," I said, softer and with the ache in my heart showing much more than I intended. "My instincts lead me down a road I can't take."

Mom's face fell. "You two are meant for each other," she said. "I knew it even when you were infants, felt the connection between you. But Quaid has chosen another path. And you must do your best to find happiness."

I refused to cry over him anymore. "It's not like I don't have a selection to choose from."

She laughed at my joke. "You can have your pick of anyone, my darling daughter," she said. "Choose wisely." Mom's expression shifted to serious. "Have you discussed it with Liam?"

"He wants to be the one," I said. Gulped down some water to douse the fire rising in my chest.

"You need to talk about it." Her eyes drifted to her wine. "I know he loves you, but does he fully understand what marrying you will mean for him?" One fingernail tinkled against the glass. "For your children?"

"We haven't yet," I said. "But you don't sound very optimistic about his answers. Does that mean you don't approve of Liam either?" Funny, didn't get my back up the way it used to, thinking he wasn't a good match for me. Probably because I was finally accepting it was true.

"Not at all," Mom said. "I will support you no matter who you marry. But Syd, don't jump into something out of need. Follow your heart. Promise me."

I nodded, leaned close to hug her. "I promise." Part of me wanted to spill my guts, to talk into the night with her about how I felt for Liam, my longing for Quaid. But from the sad look on her face, the way her lips tightened and her shoulders, too, I knew she was thinking about her own love lost.

When she looked up and met my eyes, though, she smiled. And that smile made me feel better about the whole mess.

Now I just had to figure out what my heart actually wanted.

Easy, right?

chapter thirty three

I planned to go right home. But Mom's prodding had me thinking and, finally, convinced me to stop being such a whiner and face the situation I'd created.

That Liam and I made together.

He looked surprised to see me when I pounded on his door, pushing past him and into his room, not even bothering to strip off my coat and scarf as I set my laptop bag on his bed and faced him.

"We have to talk."

From his expression, sliding from surprise to worry, he'd been dreading this as much as I had. Except he sat, offering one hand, pulling me down into his lap where I sat, stiff and shivering from emotion and stress while he stroked my hair back from my face.

"I know something has changed," he said. "I can feel it, Syd. You aren't the same with me as you were before you left." He sighed and sat back, still holding my hand and me across his thighs. "Whatever it is, whatever you have to tell me, it's okay." Hazel eyes sparked with green. "But I want you to know, if there is someone else, I'm going to fight for you as long as you'll let me." A sweet grin, crooked and charming, broke across his face. "And even after you ask me to stop."

Oh, Liam. I hugged him, resting my head on his shoulder, tension leaving me as sadness took its place.

"I just feel so trapped." I hadn't meant to whisper. Or to allow tears to rise. Stupid emotions. "And I don't want to make a mistake. Everyone is watching, speculating. Offering their own opinions."

"And none of them include me." Liam nodded before I could protest, so matter-of-fact I kissed his cheek softly in comfort. "I know your family doesn't consider me your ideal choice." He drew a breath before fixing me with a firm gaze. "I realize you would marry Quaid if he were free." Choke. "That I'm probably at the bottom of the line when it comes to husband material, because of my heritage." He bit his lower lip, the only sign of his distress. "And that you could have your pick of any witch here at college, anywhere, for that matter."

He wavered in front of me, my tears finally cresting.

"But Syd," he said, thumb swiping gently over the first of them to fall, "none of them love you like I do." He pressed my hand to his chest, his heart thudding

264

heavily under my fingers, earnestness pouring from every cell of his body. "Not one of them adores you, worships you. Will do anything, give anything, to be beside you." He kissed me oh so softly. Breathed into my mouth. "Not like I do."

I didn't think it was possible to melt. But I was melting, my insides giving way, my resistance caving in to the absolute sweetness of the handsome, loving man who held me in his arms.

"No matter what comes," he said, "what trials we face in the future, I will always be here for you, Syd. Always."

I kissed him back, not with the heat of passion, but the tenderness of real love.

"I'll have to leave you alone a lot," I said. "You'll be left behind, Liam. I have a job to do and you know I'll be in danger." Okay, so that wasn't new. His eyes told me as much. "And I'm more powerful than you." Hit him in his ego, nice work. But Liam didn't flinch.

"I've always known that," he said. "I'm not envious. Just proud."

"What about your education?" He'd talked about staying a few more years, maybe becoming a teacher himself, working at Harvard. "You'd have to give that up to look after our kids." Gulp. "The family."

"I have the archive," he said. "And teaching is highly overrated."

Sounded like he had an answer for everything.

But were they the answers I was looking for?

Liam stood, setting me on my feet while I hung my head, misery winning over even his sweet nature.

"I won't push you," he said, pressing his lips to the top of my head. "But now that I've had a taste of you, of what our lives could be like… Syd, I won't let that go easily." I forced myself to look up and meet his gaze. "I may not be perfect for you, but I'll be the best husband I can possibly be."

I bobbed a nod, not sure what to say.

If I could speak, even.

"So," he said, hands going into his back pockets as though to keep himself from touching me, "where do we go from here?" He rocked on his heels. "Are we still dating or do you need space?"

It wasn't fair to him not to give an answer.

"I don't know," I said. "I guess… we see what happens."

Coward.

I left him then, after a firm hug and his whispered "I love you" tickling my ear. The dark embraced me as I stepped out into the Yard and began my trudge home. I could have ridden the veil to my dorm, but I needed the walk to clear my head and weigh options.

Why, if I thought Liam wasn't right for me, was I having such a hard time letting go? I paused as I slammed into the answer like someone hit me in the face.

He was family. And I couldn't just push him aside. My loyalty, ingrained into me my entire life, tempered by the last few years and all the disasters I'd survived, only strengthened my need to protect those I cared about.

Even from myself. When I was the enemy.

But did that mean I was done? That Liam and I were over? No matter how I rationalized my reaction to him, I still couldn't bring myself to believe my hyperactive protectiveness was the only reason. I did love him. Loved how we were together.

Could I picture him as my husband or not?

Sighing into the cold air, I resumed walking and beating myself up.

It had snowed all day, fresh paths carved out of the heavy white stuff, weighing down the branches of the trees. I paused part way home and looked around at the crystal night sky with the pinpoints of stars just visible beyond the glare of the lights in the Yard. The waning moon casting its cold glare over the snow. Beautiful. Quiet. Everyone was inside, leaving me alone in the silence of the winter night.

Almost alone.

I knew the sound of that giggle, the squeak of boots on frosted stone. I turned to find Kristophe and Jean Marc approaching, smirks on their ugly Dumont faces.

Rage bubbled, rage for Charlotte and her people, for all those years of their humiliation, for centuries of enslavement. My magic burned inside me, ready to tear them apart.

Just push me, asshats. See how far your posing and position will take you.

To the curb. You betcha.

They came to a halt a few feet from me, under a light so Kristophe could pull one of his model poses and show off his pretty, long hair.

Charming.

"What a pity," Kristophe said with a duck-lip mew. "It seems your Sidhe bodyguard has run off, too." He rolled his eyes at his brother. "Pity how she can't seem to hang on to the help."

"Must be something they smelled." Jean Marc's heavy brows pulled together.

Kristophe tittered, one gloved hand placed artfully over his generous mouth.

"If that was supposed to hurt my feelings," I said, "you failed miserably. Just like at everything else the Dumont family tries to do."

And snap.

They both looked shocked by my response, then a little afraid. Well, hell yeah. They should be afraid of me, the nasty little weasels.

Hang on. I wasn't that scary. Not enough they both backed off a step. Moved closer to each other, mouths hanging open.

"Hello, Jean Marc." A familiar voice drifted over my right shoulder, light and sweet in the stillness of the dark. "And my very dear Kristophe." Charlotte came to stand next to me, a deliciously pert smile on her face. "How lovely to see you both again under such auspicious circumstances."

Neither of them said a word as I gaped at her right along with them.

"I've been looking forward to our reunion." She drifted closer to the brothers, her power humming around her, reaching for them and not in a pleasant way.

"Back off, werewolf." Jean Marc's attempt at bravado fell so flat even he winced.

Charlotte's laugh tinkled in the cold air. "I'll allow you that one slip," she said, magic pulsing with fire and the thrum of the earth. "For old time's sake." The way she said it, the burst of fear on their faces, made me wonder just what they had done to her all those years she was their slave. Reminded me of Kristophe's parting remark about the lessons he taught her. "But from now on, you can address me as 'Your Highness'."

Can I get a whoop-whoop?

The brothers exchanged a look before backing off another step. A stride, really.

Charlotte cocked her head to the side. "What, going so soon? We have so much to catch up on. And I have so much to repay you."

I giggled into my hands as the pair turned their yellow bellies and ran like rabbits.

Charlotte turned back to me, a huge smile on her face. "That," she said, "was very satisfying."

"I bet." I hugged her hard, her arms winding around me. "Missed you."

"You too." Charlotte leaned back, teeth flashing as she grinned at me. "You look wonderful."

I always adored Charlotte, but this new version was even more awesome. "You too. How are things going back home?"

She shrugged, linking her arm in mine, turning me toward my dorm. "Fine, I suppose. But my life is much better," she said with a quaver in her happy voice. "Now that I'm back where I belong."

Um, what? I stopped us dead, staring again. Charlotte bounced on her toes, her excitement as clear as a kid's at Christmas. "Silly," she said, tears in her beautiful eyes, "what family did you think I was talking about when we had that conversation?"

I couldn't stop the sob that burst from me as I hugged her again.

"I might be heir," she whispered as we both laughed and cried in the snowy night. "But you are my real family."

I pulled back from her, wiping at my wet cheeks. "On one condition," I said.

"Name it." Her mittens dried her own face.

"No more bodywere." I hooked my arm through hers as she'd done to me just a moment earlier.

She smiled. Nodded.

"Friends," we said together. I forgot Liam, my obligations, the upcoming wedding, my battle with the Brotherhood. Charlotte was home.

Charlotte was *home*.

We laughed our way back to my dorm to tell Shenka the good news.

CHAPTER THIRTY FOUR

And life, as complicated as it was, went on.

And on.

The Steam Union never did uncover Vasyl, so I figured he'd show up again when I least expected. Because, yeah. That was the way things rolled for me.

Piers went to great lengths to keep me up to date on the trial of the Black Souls and the continuing Vasyl hunt, though, so he had lots of opportunities to just show up and make himself available. With lots of suggestive comments and kissing thrown in for good measure.

At least I'd managed to keep him from running into Liam. So far. Wasn't looking forward to that disaster if it ever happened.

I'd seen jealous Liam before, and it wasn't a performance I wanted him to repeat.

The worst part was I knew I could send Piers away at

any time. But I didn't want to. And that made me a truly wretched human being and a despicable girlfriend. Though I wasn't much of the latter lately, to my credit. Despite our conversation, his assurance he would never stop trying, I pulled away from Liam completely, at least when it came to a physical relationship. A hasty decision was the last thing I needed. He didn't like it, but, in typical Liam fashion, he didn't complain. Stopped hovering after a few weeks. Gave me my space, though the tragic and hurt looks I caught on his face from time to time nearly drove me into his arms to comfort him.

Which would have been a massive mistake. Comforting would have led to kissing and kissing to… well. As much as the memory of the lovely weekend we spent together made me tingle all over when I let my mind linger on it, I was still so at odds with myself, the stress giving me almost constant heartburn, I actually walked in the opposite direction sometimes when I saw him approaching just so I didn't have to fake a smile and pretend at friendship.

I missed him. I loved him. But I couldn't go there yet.

I felt like now I'd experience what life would be with him I had to reexamine my preconceived notions of what marriage to him would be like.

And I wasn't sure I was in love with that picture.

Yes, it meant I was doing exactly to him what Quaid had done to me. Guilty. Which made me empathize with

Quaid.

Damn him.

As for Piers, he was hot, available and he wanted me. I didn't love him—at least, not yet—but did that matter?

Sigh.

On a happier couple note, Isabelle and her wereboy, Maksym, were together at last. She was allowed to handle her father's body, Sunny not caring really what happened to Yure now he was dead. I did hear rumblings of resentment from her werewolves about it. There were a few suggestions floating around about desecrating his body. And while I understood their anger and need for some semblance of revenge, Charlotte firmly put an end to the simmering anger by tromping on toes.

Hard.

And was kind enough to bring me with her to watch the show.

She was so considerate like that.

After Sunny invited the werewolf to live in Austria with his vampire girlfriend, Maksym accepted, a few of his friends choosing to go with him. Though, from what Charlotte told me, Oleksander wasn't exactly happy about the vampire queen poaching some of his people so soon after their liberation.

At least now that the connection to sorcery was broken, the natural animosity between werewolves and vampires had disappeared. Not that it canceled out years of racism. But at least werewolves and vampires could occupy the same room and not try to kill each other.

As often.

I knew it would take a lot for the werewolves to adjust their attitudes. They'd been trained as bullies and such training would be hard to break. But Oleksander ruled with a steel fist and a good heart, Charlotte their idol they adored and worshiped, so I had faith the werewolves would be all right.

My one instance I was invited to be a werewolf/vampire mediator, held on common ground at the old coven site in Wilding Springs, went much better than I expected with only minimal shouting and accusations on both sides, so I counted it a win.

And would never do it again.

It became obvious someone was still running the Russian mafia, so I felt sure the Brotherhood had their hands deeper in Yure's pies than he'd known. I let things ride, not like I could do much, anyway. With Applegate firmly closing her borders to all witches and prodding Mom almost constantly about my continuing visits to Europe, I knew it would be a long time before the Brotherhood would be ousted from her territory.

If ever.

Charlotte and I returned to her home quite frequently, and openly. I refused to cloak my power despite Applegate's boundaries, and knew it had to be burning away at Liander Belaisle he couldn't do a thing about it. But Charlotte had to be available. She was still princess, after all, and doing an excellent job. All the werewolves looked up to her so much I couldn't help but grin like a proud momma.

Like I had something to do with how awesome she'd turned out.

Mom told me Applegate finally gave up trying to stop me from crossing her territory using official channels and to watch my back. Like I didn't already. Between the two of us, we were keeping a close eye on all sorcery. It became commonplace for me to sweep any room I entered just in case.

Nervous times.

I ran into Mia occasionally, my worry for her taking a side seat to everything else. But her growing fanaticism and clear instability made me feel nervous.

And guilty.

Weirdly, Shenka treated the former Dumont with something close to disgust whenever she showed up. I was shocked at first. My second seemed so level headed and acted kindly toward everyone. But there was something rubbing her the wrong way when it came to my old Goth friend.

I let it pass. We had more important things to think about than one damaged witch girl.

Like the fact we only had three months of school left.

And then I graduated college. Moved home for good. Had my—gulp—twenty-first birthday.

Got married.

Lived happily ever after.

Yeah. Right.

Because me and happily ever after were best friends.

Like what you read? Find out more at
pattilarsen.com

Here's a look at the first chapter of
Book Eighteen of the Hayle Coven Novels

ENFORCER

chapter one

I lifted the tea cup to my lips in an effort to hide the scowl threatening to turn my fake smile into a grimace of anguish.

Huan Wong, Santos Council member, sat across from me, her round cheeks flushed as she fixed her narrow eyes on my empty left hand.

Considering the fact it was August and my twenty-first birthday had come and gone months ago, I knew the absence of a wedding band was the main reason for this little visit from the High Council.

That's right. The entire High Council of North American Witches sat in my living room, sipping tea from Mom's china while I ground my teeth together in an effort to keep from kicking the lot of them out of my house.

It's not like I wasn't expecting this visit. Mom warned

me long before now I'd have a price to pay for ducking my head and barreling through my birthday at Beltane, June, July and now part of August in clear rebellion of Council law. I was supposed to be married by now.

Grumble, mumble.

Freakout.

"Not to put it indelicately, Sydlynn," Willa Rhodes said, clearing her throat as her cup tinkled on her saucer, a drip of tea washing over the edge to stain the flat of the white plate. "But you have put your coven in a terrible position." The old witch's face scrunched in an apologetic smile.

The Council members all nodded while Mom held her peace, calmly nibbling a little sandwich Shenka hastily prepared for our unexpected guests.

Thank goodness for my second and her fast-on-her-feet abilities. I'd have stared stupidly at them in the kitchen if it hadn't been for her. She took the entire thing in hand, guiding the Council into the living room, seating me graciously, while wrangling all the nitty gritty details as my temper simmered under their stares.

Tea seemed to have diffused some of their agitation, but it was clear I wasn't getting out of this with a little hot sugar and milk and a handful of crustless snacks.

And yet, Mom's relaxed state gave me more confidence than perhaps I should have had. I learned a long time ago to follow her lead. And since I had my real mother back, I could trust that lead more now than ever.

"I've studied the law," I said, grateful Shenka suggested it. Panic set in about two weeks before the big day, so powerful and all-consuming I almost ran to Demonicon to hide from the inevitability of wedding bells.

How was I supposed to just choose? Liam and I were still a little distant, all my fault. I had, as of yet, to commit to the love he professed, freaked out to no end by the thought of making the wrong choice. And though the handsome and charming Piers Southway pressed his case on a regular basis, I didn't love the Steam Union sorcerer. And wasn't sure he'd be a good fit for the coven anyway.

Excuses. Enough I talked myself into a frenzy of flight, only to be pinned down by my faithful second who shoved a copy of coven law under my quivering nose and offered a solution.

Temporary, yes. But a solution nonetheless.

Erica's eyes widened as she set her cup aside, glancing sideways at Mom. "The law is clear, Syd," she said, blonde hair, once a cute bob, now grown out to rival my mother's long black locks. "And you've broken it. We've pushed our willingness to accept a little leeway, but with the approach of conclave..." She sat back as the others—minus Mom—murmured their agreement.

So that's what this was about. *They're worried about saving face?* I sent the tight mental question to Mom.

Witches are always worried about appearances, she sent with a heavy dose of amusement in her voice.

Nice to see someone was finding my imminent doom funny.

Just tell them what you discovered, Mom sent. *I'll do my best to back you up. But don't hold your breath.*

Shenka refilled my cup with steady hands, her pleasant smile far more natural than she had the right to. Her dark eyes met mine, her calm as comforting as Mom's.

Breathe, Syd. Just breathe. "According to law," I said, "I have until my twenty-first birthday to marry if I want to remain coven leader. Correct?"

The assembled ladies nodded, murmuring their agreement.

"Actually," I said, stomach quivering with butterflies as I delivered the punchline, "that's not quite accurate." Shenka lifted the scroll of law from the end table and handed it to me like a magical Vanna White, all prepped and perky.

My lovely assistant.

I unrolled the scroll to the place she'd marked for me, speaking out loud while I read, the words rising to etch in blue fire in the air as I did.

"'And it shall be that all Coven Leaders wed well and true, in the year of their twenty first.'"

The words burned over my left shoulder, solid,

unwavering.

"Yes," Huan said. "Precisely."

"No," I said. "I think you missed it." I pushed my power against the hovering script. "In the year of" popped out, bigger and brighter. "According to this, I still have nine months to find a suitable partner and wed."

Phew. I already felt lighter now I'd said it out loud.

Willa frowned, head tilted as she stared at the floating words, but Huan spluttered out some tea.

"You are purposely misconstruing the letter of the law," she said.

"No," I said, tossing the scroll into her lap. "I'm following it. To the word." Clearly no one ever contested it. I guess I was the only person who actually thought it was nuts to make me marry at such a young age.

Witches were crazypants.

Mom's mind hugged mine. *You made your point*, she sent. *Let me handle this.*

Happy to.

"An interesting interpretation," Mom said.

"You would think so," Huan bit at her, bitterness heavy in her voice.

Mom's blue eyes pierced the Santos Council member, her faint smile gone in a flash, face now cold and blank. "Are you accusing me of something, Council Member Santos?"

Huan backed down immediately, head bowing. "Not

283

at all, Council Leader," she said, though her hands twitched around the scroll like she wanted to attack me with it.

"I'm afraid I have to side with Sydlynn on this one," Willa said. I felt my stomach loosen, the knot releasing. Willa and her sister, Coven Leader Violet Rhodes, were both sticklers for the law. "I have to confess, I've never read this particular passage myself. But it appears, as Sydlynn states, we've been misinterpreting it for centuries."

Holy. Did I just win?

From the angry looks on the Council member's faces, Willa's opinion wasn't appreciated.

"Coven Leader Hayle has done more for this Council and all witches than any other in her few short years," Mom said. "For that reason, we have allowed her leeway in her marriage choice and timing." Whoa. Choice? Were they planning on saddling me with someone they picked or something?

My demon snarled, Shaylee's power rumbling far beneath the house even as my vampire hissed in outrage. The family magic swirled in protest, though I did my best to hide my unhappiness from the Council.

We'd see how long someone they chose for me survived.

Mom went on, her mind chuckling in mine. Because she clearly knew where my thoughts were.

"For now, I agree with her assessment of the law as well, bending to the input of Council Member Rhodes." Instant protest, though Willa nodded to Mom. My mother held up one hand as I scowled at Erica for being a traitor. So much for old family ties. "However, I understand the importance of Coven Leader Hayle's marriage." *I'm sorry, sweetheart*, Mom sent. *But it really is important.* "While I know many of you would prefer she married before conclave, it is obvious, the very event now only days away, she won't be wed by then."

They scowled at me as a group. What, were they going to drop off some guy, zippity do da me down the aisle and present me, officially hitched, to the rest of the World Councils?

So not going to happen in my lifetime.

"The very fact one of our most powerful coven leaders,"—one of? Seriously—"blatantly flaunts the fact she thinks herself outside the law makes our position on the international stage all the more precarious." Huan's lips pinched into a straight line, her straight, black hair swinging as she shook her head. "And while I'm as grateful to her as anyone," sure she was, "this kind of defiance is unconscionable."

"I seem to recall," I shot back, "I was granted carte blanche by this very Council."

That shut them up.

But Mom sighed, shattering my little advantage.

"While we have granted you the freedom to act in our best interest," she said, "your marriage isn't included in that agreement, Coven Leader Hayle."

She just had to hack the floor out from under me, didn't she?

Huan lurched to her feet, face set in a mask of anger. "I for one am embarrassed at this state of affairs," she said. Turned on Mom. "And I insist the Council act on the problem before it becomes a larger issue." She returned her gaze to me. "I would hate to see you forced to step down as coven leader of the Hayle family."

Such. A. Liar. She was in bed far enough with the Dumonts I was sure she'd be happy to see me fall. Her old allegiance with Odette, the now deceased leader of that hated family, couldn't have ended with the matriarch's fall. In fact, I had no doubt the Santos coven was still heavily invested with the Dumonts, especially now that Odette's son, Andre, was coven leader.

"I'm certain Sydlynn will make the proper choice," Mom said, rising to her feet with a gracious nod to Shenka and I. "And in time to fulfill the letter of our law."

The others rose, nodded to me, Shenka leading them out. I stayed where I was, swiping in irritation at the still floating letters hanging beside me, popping each word like a bubble while blue sparks fell to the floor.

Damn it.

Just damn it.

Mom sat next to me as the sounds of Shenka saying goodbye echoed from the kitchen. Her hands reached for mine, her power hugging me.

"I'm sorry, Mom," I said. "I hate to put you in this position."

"You too, sweetheart," Mom said. "This excuse of yours will only last so long. I doubt they will allow you to go the full year. It's been a battle to make it this far."

"Thanks for backing me up." I sagged against the puffy armrest of the sofa, feeling defeated. "I just have no idea what I'm going to do."

A fat, silver body landed in my lap as Sassafras, my demon Persian, settled himself against me, amber eyes on fire.

"Interesting conversation," he said. Eavesdropper. "Do you have to be so stubborn or are you enjoying yourself?"

Smartass cat. "Okay then," I said to him. "Who would you pick if you were me?"

He sniffed, swiping one paw over his nose. "I'm not you," he said.

Argh.

"See," I turned to Mom as Shenka sat across from us, "this is the help I get."

"No one can make this decision for you," Mom said. Paused. Bit her lower lip. "Have you talked to Quaid?"

Oh. My. Swearword. She did so not bring him up just now.

"No," I snarled through my aching jaw.

We were meant for each other. If he hadn't chosen a life with the Enforcers, cutting off any chance we had to be together, he would be my first and only choice.

But no. Quaid was out.

And I couldn't bear to pick someone else.

I hated how weak that made me feel.

"Stop being so picky." I spun at the sound of Gram's voice, staring as she scowled at me. But not my familiar Gram, not the powerful woman full of vigor and snark. This old lady with the withered skin and fluffy white hair looked petulant, reduced. Felt that way, too. And had since Ameline Benoit stole her magic a year ago.

Magic I promised Gram I'd get back for her. Except I couldn't, could I? Not while I needed Ameline and her dark maji self to defeat the Brotherhood.

Guilt.

"Gram," I said. "You were the one who told me how important this was—"

She swatted the air in front of her, frown so deep her brows almost touched in the center of her forehead.

"Get on with it," she grumped. "Hurry the hell up and pick one already." She turned, shuffled a step. "They're all the same anyway."

I watched her go, heart aching, wishing I had my

Gram back. When I returned my attention to the others, they all watched me, expectant.

And the pressure of their expectation was way too heavy for me to bear.

"I'll pick," I said, standing, dumping Sassafras on Mom. "But I won't be pushed into it."

I know it wasn't fair to be angry with my mother, my cat, my best friend.

Or myself.

Life wasn't fair sometimes.

aboUt the aUthor

Everything you need to know about me is in this one
statement: I've wanted to be a writer since I was a little
girl, and now I'm doing it. How cool is that, being able to
follow your dream and make it reality? I've tried
everything from university to college, graduating the
second with a journalism diploma (I sucked at telling real
stories), am part of an all-girl improv troupe (if you've
never tried it, I highly recommend making things up as
you go along as often as possible). I've even been in a
Celtic girl band (some of our stuff is on YouTube!) and
was an independent film maker. My life has been one
creative thing after another—all leading me here, to
writing books for a living.

Now with multiple series in happy publication, I live on beautiful and magical Prince Edward Island (I know you've heard of Anne of Green Gables) with my very patient husband and multitude of pets.

I love-love-love hearing from you! You can reach me (and I promise I'll message back) at patti@pattilarsen.com. And if you're eager for your next dose of Patti Larsen books (usually about one release a month) come join my mailing list! All the best up and coming, giveaways, contests and, of course, my observations on the world (aren't you just dying to know what I think about everything?) all in one place: http://smarturl.it/PattiLarsenEmail.

Last—but not least!—I hope you enjoyed what you read! Your happiness is my happiness. And I'd love to hear just what you thought. A review where you found this book would mean the world to me—reviews feed writers more than you will ever know. So, loved it (or not so much), **your honest review would make my day**. Thank you!